# 13:55 Eastern Standard Time

## *And Other Stories*

# Nick Alexander

# Nick Alexander

Nick Alexander was born in 1964 in the UK. He has travelled widely and has lived and worked both in the UK. and the USA. He currently lives with two cats and four goldfish in Nice, France.

Nick is the editor of the bi-monthly satirical news site www.BIGfib.com

*13:55 Eastern Standard Time* is his fourth fictional work. His previous trilogy comprising, *50 Reasons to Say Goodbye, Sottopassaggio* and *Good Thing, Bad Thing*, is also available from BIGfib Books. For more information, to contact the author, or to order extra copies please visit his website on www.nick-alexander.com

# Acknowledgements

Thanks to Fay Weldon for encouraging me when it most counted. Thanks to Rosemary and Dave for all their encouragement, to John Dalton for his helpful comments, to Edwin Soon for his help with the Chinese, and to Grenville Godfrey and Richard Labonte for their proofing skills.

## Legal Notice

ISBN: 2-9524899-6-3 / ISBN13: 9-7829-5248-9966

*"Cause and effect, means and ends,
seed and fruit cannot be severed;
for the effect already blooms in the cause,
the end pre-exists in the means,
the fruit in the seed."*

**– Ralph Waldo Emerson**

# Part One

*"We are never alone.*
*We are all aspects of one great being.*
*No matter how far apart we are, the air links us."*

**— Yoko Ono**

# OK Sticker

Hua Juan straightens her back. They like the back to be straight – it indicates attentiveness. She takes the next box from the conveyor and places it in the slot. The screen lights up with the colours of the rainbow and a noise, like a police car siren – only constant – sounds in the headphones.

She pulls the box from the slot and sticks a white OK sticker on the shiny back cover, then reaches behind her and places it on another conveyor. Her movements are fluid and elegant. She glances along the conveyor and notices again how different everyone's movements are. Hui, her friend, moves jerkily. Juan always thinks she looks like she is trying to impress the foreman – trying to look fast. But she moves the same way outside the factory too, so it must just be the way she is.

Her hand reaches forward describing a graceful arc, and swipes another box from the belt. Her name, Juan, means graceful, and she wonders if her parents chose the name because they somehow *knew* that she would be graceful, or if she *became* so *because* of the name she was given. She wonders about many such things during the long days in front of the belt. She likes the fact that her mind is free even if her body is a prisoner, here, beneath the strip lights on this hard stool.

Sound in both ears, no dark lines on the screen – she sticks another OK sticker and places the box behind her. This is a good batch – she likes it when the boxes are all the same, either good or bad. It lets her settle into a rhythm, the movements become like ballet. It's when the boxes are all different – some good, some bad – that it gets hard. You have to start thinking about what you're doing.

Hua Juan doesn't really know what the boxes are for. She knows she only has to ask, but she has worked in many factories, and she knows that understanding doesn't always help. In her last job she found out that she was spending fifteen hours a day making parts for a Japanese egg timer that made a chicken noise when the egg was cooked. For some reason, knowing this had depressed her, until she couldn't concentrate anymore. Her error rate was too high then, and they had sacked her.

She lifts and connects, scans the screen and listens, sticks on a sticker and thinks of Yaaja. It will be time for the harvest soon, and she wonders if it has been a good growing year. Her parents will be out in the beautiful fields. Yaaja is stunning at dawn – rice fields in the plain, deep and green and perfumed, maize on the higher ground. Mists lie low across the rice fields in the mornings – the sight took her breath away every time. They will be cutting the corn cobs soon; her grandmother will be drying the husks as fuel for the winter.

The last year she spent at home – three years ago – was terrible. The year was too dry and the corn was half the usual size. They had nothing to sell to the cooperative and even the husks were too small – they ended up burning grass-bricks for heat. It had been a long cold winter.

Life is better here in Longhua. The dormitories are warm, and they have hot showers and free meals but she still misses… She thinks about *what* she misses – obviously her family, though in truth she has more fun with the girls in the dorm than she ever did at home. But more than anything it's the passing of time, the marking of the seasons that she misses. Planting, harvesting, preparing for winter. Here every day is the same, she hardly sees the weather. It's like living in a dream. She knows she will return to the land.

No sound on the right. She drops the box into the reject bin. No sound on the right. Another one. Black line on screen. She places it in the defective screen box and peers down the line. Ou-Yang Hui looks up at her and shrugs as she too drops a box into the reject bin. She likes Ou-Yang Hui. Her husband used to beat her, which is sad. She has one eye permanently closed. She's so funny, has such a great sense of humour. How could anyone do that?

Hua Juan narrows her eyes and tightens her lips. If these faults carry on then production will stop, and there will be no overtime today. She wouldn't mind so much. Yesterday was a long day – eighteen hours, but she needs the money too. She needs to save as much as she can while she still has time.

Ahh. She sighs with relief and relaxes her shoulders. Two of the boxes in a row are OK. Then three. Then four. She settles back into her rhythm.

Yes, every day here is the same, the endless procession of little white boxes marching down the belt. She likes the boxes. She likes the rainbow picture when she plugs them in; she likes the rounded corners. They look somehow *friendly*.

The only thing that changes here is the hours – most days fourteen, but sometimes as many as eighteen. Once, when they were behind because of production problems, they worked for twenty-two hours in a row.

It was hard, but it's good. She needs the money. And it won't last, so she likes the overtime days. As long as they don't all come in a row. Then they get too tiring. Then her back aches and she can't sleep and she's even more tired the next day.

But she will be sacked when they find out. So overtime is good.

These are all fine now, a good batch. Yes, she likes it when they all come through the same. Her motions become automatic: reach, slot, look, listen, stick, reach, slot, look, listen...

She wonders how Sun Lee is doing. She wonders what he will say when he finds out. Sun Lee, her oldest childhood friend. She used to think they would marry one day. She wouldn't have minded – he grew up into a handsome man. But she had to leave and then he got a girl from the next village pregnant. Chan Xia. She is pretty, but, Juan thinks, a little stupid. But Lee seems happy. They have a beautiful son; they called him Liang, which simply means *Good*. And he is. Sun Lee was very happy to have a boy. A son is better for helping on the land and bringing wealth to the family.

But then girls can do that too these days. That's why she's here. She flushes with pride at the two hundred Yuan she has been sending home every month. Her mother says they would never have got through the winter without it.

She receives a hard slap on the shoulder, and automatically sits up straight. She glances behind at the foreman who is glaring at her, already walking on down the aisle. "*See-feut-loong*," she thinks. – Asshole. *He thinks he is so important strutting in his uniform, but he is nobody.*

She looks at the clock, and then down the line where the boxes advance towards her. There is no sign of them slowing, so today will be an overtime day.

Her back aches more when she sits straight. The belt is too low really – or the stool too high. It gets a little harder every day. She thinks about the coming days, the rumours, the scandal, the interviews with the Party people, the free "healthcare" offers, and she wonders again if she is strong enough to resist. She thinks she is, but so many girls cave in – it makes you wonder.

Lian on the top bunk said she would never abort, but they shut her in the interview room for four hours and when she came out she had changed her mind. She still says she's glad, still says she's too young to have a baby, but Hua Juan has heard her crying at night. Ou-Yang Dai actually told her to shut up two nights ago. But Ou-Yang Dai is a heartless bitch. She would make a good foreman.

So yes, she needs the money. She's sending home half her earnings. And through not going out with the other girls she's been managing to save half the rest. And Cheung, she smiles as she thinks of Cheung, her heart aches as she thinks of his beautiful face, of the way he smiles at her, yes, Cheung says he will stay here in the Longhua factory until the baby is born. Cheung has no family now, so he is saving everything. Poor Cheung. No family – floating un-tethered like a balloon. But she will give him a family. They will take this emptiness and fill it with happiness. They will create it from nothing and it will hold him down, stop him floating away. She wonders what her life will be like once they have a baby. They don't know yet quite how they can earn a living and be together, but she has faith that it will happen somehow.

She thinks about the possibilities – a girl or a boy. Secretly she would rather a girl, but she knows Cheung would like a son. As only children themselves, they are allowed to have two children, so they can always try again.

So, no, she won't be one of the girls who changes her mind. She just has to think of Cheung, floating like a balloon, and she knows that she won't. She will be one of the girls who loses her job instead.

No red on the screen. She drops it into the box. No sound on the left. Into the box.

She sighs. The faults have dragged her back into the here and now. She looks at the clock, and checks down the conveyor to see if there is any sign of the day ending.

Another slap on the shoulder, only this time the foreman pulls the headphone away from her ear.

"Stand up," he shouts. "Feun kou tim yong tak chou Pod leh?" – *How is Pod made if you are asleep?*

She obeys and he drags the stool away to the wall behind her. "iPod hai ghaim ghiam yaer," he continues, walking away. – *iPod is a precision thing.*

"Sorry," she says. "I will give it my full attention."

She repositions the headphone over her ear and shifts her weight from one foot to the other.

She looks down at her belly – nothing showing yet, but it won't be long. Maybe another month. Unless the "doctor" comes round with the ultrasound again. That can happen any time, you just never know. But maybe she'll be lucky. Later is better. Later means more money for the baby, more money for grandmother's medicine.

She glances down the line. Hui catches her eye, winks discreetly and drops an iPod into the reject box. She smiles at her friend's solidarity and shifts her weight to the other foot. Now her back is really hurting.

She hears a noise beyond the headphones and peeps across the shop floor. The foreman has taken away another girl's stool. "*Saur kow,*" she thinks. – Stupid dog! She's only a new girl.

She wonders how they can be so mean, the foremen. They have all worked on the conveyor; they know what it's like. But they put on a *Hon Hai* uniform and strut up and down the line, and suddenly think they are powerful. But they are nothing. They are dust!

No sound on the right. She sticks an OK sticker on the back of the box and places it on the conveyor belt behind her. It could get her into trouble, but by the time trouble comes she'll be long gone. As long as she keeps her promise. No sound on the right again. Another OK sticker. Yes, she promises herself that she will be long gone.

Nothing registers on her face, but deep down she smiles to herself. *"These dogs have no power over me,"* she thinks. *"No power at all."*

She wonders if the warmth she is feeling, deep down inside … well, she wonders if it is the baby smiling.

# Eight Million

A lice stands and stares at the shiny streets of the city below, then pulls back her focal point and watches as the droplets of rain chase each other down the pane. "Eight million," she says quietly. She leans forward and rests her forehead against the glass. It is cold and unyielding, uncomfortable and hard. And yet... And yet, in some strange way the discomfort comforts her. It almost pierces the bubble – almost breaks through the numbness.

She sighs heavily and straightens her back, then raises a hand to support herself. Three yellow cabs slither along the street below.

She turns from the window and looks back into the room. The light is fading and she should switch on some lamps. Or go out.

She could go and sit in the bar again. The waiter was friendly enough. She could sit there until another freak starts trying to buy her a drink and then come home again. She could maybe try another bar. But the barman might not chat to her. Or the freaks could be worse. They usually are.

She throws herself onto the sofa and pulls the remote from beneath her buttocks. *TV.* It takes away the pain. But it doesn't solve anything.

She wonders – again – what would happen if she got rid of the TV. Would her life be different? Would some process be unleashed – the boredom building until it got *so* bad that... Maybe that would *make* things change? Maybe it would get so bad that something would just *have* to happen? Or would she just sit and stare at the wall. Would she just go out of her mind?

She tips her head back and looks up at the ceiling, listening to the sounds of hard shoes on the floor above. "*Eight million!*" she thinks.

There are people above her, forty floors of them, and below her feet, another nine floors. There are people just beyond the wall to her right, left, behind her. There are people everywhere except here. She glances at the window, at the thousands of squares of light opposite and wonders if behind one of those squares, somewhere in New York city, another person is sitting – another person as lonely, as *desperate* for company as she is right now.

She looks at her bookcase, but she's not in the mood for reading, not in the mood for poetry. She sighs and fingers the remote again. Her finger lingers over the large orange power button.

So many nights watching TV – nights in New York, and before those, nights in Alabama.

She thought moving would change everything. She thought that getting rid of the yards of lawn around her, of swapping them for these thin walls would change something. She thought giving up the silent bubble of her daily drive to work in the Ford – of trading it for the bustle and squash of the subway would break her isolation. Once and for all.

And of course, everything *has* changed. There are people above, below, behind her – inches away. She no longer listens to 987 Kiss as she drives to work – she listens to her Walkman instead. She glances at it lying dead beside her. Listen*ed*. Even Japanese products die one day.

She scans the room and her eyes settle on the new red refrigerator. It's a beautiful object. Rounded and substantial and friendly. There's nothing inside – just a deli-box and some Chardonnay – but she knows why she bought it. The refrigerator is part of the dream.

*She opens the door – it's brimming with fresh produce. She pulls fillets of fish from the top shelf, some broccoli and mushrooms from the second, and starts to rinse the vegetables and throw them into a wok. One of her friends, for a whole bunch of them are here, counting on her for dinner – she's famed for her cooking – offers to refill her glass. She cooks and drinks and they laugh and joke about. Someone puts some music on. They eat, chatting about books and films; the food is great. Then maybe they go out for drinks. Or maybe one of the friends is a guy. Maybe one of them is her guy. When everyone has gone, maybe they have sex on the kitchen worktop.*

That image, the image of the life she thought she would have – the life she *believed*, that *Rhoda* told her was her birthright, that *Friends* and *Sex and the City* confirmed – is so vivid it pains her like the memory of a lost friend. She feels actual bereavement for the loss. But she never *had* that life. Friends never *did* just drop by. Not even here. And that seems worse. It seems to indicate some very personal failing, surely, the fact of being alone in a city of eight million people.

She stands and crosses the room to the kitchen; yanks open the heavy red door. The deli-box awaits her hunger; the wine chills, ready to soothe. She pulls the bottle from the door.

Another weekend alone. Another weekend where she probably won't speak to anyone from now until Monday. Unless she phones someone – maybe Miriam in Boston, or her mother in Wisconsin. Maybe Michael – her brother – in Berlin. *And what the fuck is Michael doing in Berlin?* she wonders. And how did that *happen?* How did the world change so that everyone got to be so far away?

Tomorrow she might speak to someone in a store, exchange a few words. Yes, she could go shopping tomorrow, if she can think of something she needs. She scans the contents of the apartment. Sofa – new, table – new, telephone, LCD TV, TiVo – all new. Even something she wants, something she *vaguely* fancies, some frivolous pointless object would do the trick.

She pulls the cork from the bottle, and returns to the sofa. She hits the orange button. The screen fills with trendy silhouettes dancing around on a colourful background. These people, these dancing silhouettes are happy grooving around with their headphones on. *They* don't need other people.

"*That's what I can do,*" she thinks. "*Get one of those and spend the weekend loading my music in; listen to it on the subway on my way to work.*" She sips her wine and feels a little better. She has a project for tomorrow.

"A thousand songs in your pocket," says the ad. The commercial break ends. Alice takes a sip, then another, then refills her glass and settles more deeply into the sofa.

Rhoda walks onscreen. The camera zooms in. Rhoda's earrings don't match. Her friends and the studio audience all laugh. Alice smiles, despite herself.

**13:55 EASTERN STANDARD TIME**

# 13:55 Eastern Standard Time

Alice stands in line. She scans the glowing whiteness of the store, checks out the people, almost exclusively men, dotted around the place. She looks at the youngsters behind the counter: dreadlocks, pierced ears, ripped jeans – even the guy in the suit has somehow managed to make it look dishevelled. She feels suddenly old and dowdy. She wonders if her clothing choices haven't become a little too conservative. She wonders when the people in these places started looking like artists instead of like geeks.

The queue shuffles forward. She glances over her shoulder. The guy behind has to be her age, but he's dressed like the people here. He has a pair of those twisted-seam jeans and an orange T-shirt with *Grotesque* written across it. It's probably the name of a band. She should probably know that.

He pulls a tight-lipped but friendly smile at her and she snaps her head back to face the front of the line and blushes. He probably thinks she's eyeing him up.

The line moves forward and the guy with dreadlocks steps forward to serve her.

"Hiya," he says. "What can I do for you ma'am?"

He's only trying to be cute, but the *ma'am* makes her feel even older.

"I bought this earlier this morning," she says, pulling the iPod from her bag. "There's no music in one ear," she explains with a shrug.

The guy nods in time with the music that's playing throughout the store and pushes his lips out. "Dead channel, huh?" he says.

"Excuse me?" It's the man behind, trying to jump the line. She hates people who just can't wait their turn. *How can anyone get to their thirties without learning even the basic element of discipline that is waiting in line?* she wonders. She opens her mouth to rebuke him.

"I couldn't help overhearing," he says. "I also have no sound on one side, picked it up just an hour ago."

*Dreadlocks* continues to nod his head. "Weird huh?" he says. He nods towards the far corner. "If you two dudes wanna go chat with the guys in the Genius Bar, they'll fix you up."

Alice frowns. She doesn't *want* to chat to someone in the Genius Bar, and she doesn't want to be called a *dude*. And she doesn't want to go with this other *dude* either. She wants this adolescent, who – she is now noticing – has zits, to exchange her brand new non-functioning iPod for a brand new *functioning* iPod.

"They'll swap them for new, right?" asks the guy in the *Grotesque* T-shirt.

*Dreadlocks* continues to nod. "Sure thing," he says, looking already to the next customer.

*Grotesque* shrugs at her cutely and holds a hand out to indicate that she should go first.

Alice forces a smile and heads off.

The genius has an incongruous piercing through his nose. He doesn't really pull off the arty-look of his colleagues. He looks like someone from a bank, only with a piercing through his nose.

"Hi there," he says, glancing at the two boxes they have placed on the counter. "iPod hassles huh?"

Alice tries to remember which words the guy used. It sounded better than her, "No music in one ear."

"We both have dead channels," *Grotesque* tells him.

*Genius* raises an eyebrow. "Both of you? That's bad luck," he says. "Gimme five." He sweeps away with the boxes.

*Grotesque* grins cutely at her. "They're so busy being cool," he says with a shake of his head and a crossing of the eyes.

Alice slips into a smile and blinks slowly. "Yeah," she says with a nod of her head. "It would be cooler if the product worked. I feel like saying, *hey, you just work in a store*, you know?"

*Grotesque* grins and holds out his hand. "Will," he says. "William ... but everyone calls me Will."

Alice shakes his hand. "Alice," she says. "Everyone just calls me Alice."

Will grins. "That accent sounds real familiar. Where you from?"

Alice smiles. "Alabama," she says. "Is that bad?"

Will shakes his head. "I like it," he says. "You remind me of my sister. She lives in Birmingham."

"You remind me of my brother actually," Alice says. "But he lives in Berlin."

Will nods, impressed. "Germany, wow."

There's a moment of silence. Alice stares at her feet and tries to think of something to say. "It's OK here though," she says. "I guess it's nicer than Wal-Mart."

Will grins. "Ain't that so," he says. "So how long have you been in New York?" He runs a hand through his hair. His silver ring glints.

"Oh, not long. Only a couple months."

"Enjoying it?"

Alice hesitates. There's nothing more unattractive than not enjoying someone else's city.

Will laughs. "I guess not huh?"

Alice shrugs. "It just takes time," she says. "To settle in and stuff."

"You have friends here?" Will asks.

Alice shakes her head and wrinkles her nose. "Work colleagues," she says. "But, you know … it's kinda hard. You think … in such a big place…"

Will nods. "My boyfriend – his name's Jude – he moved here, like, a year ago. And he gets real lonely. And, I mean, he's got me, and my friends, but, well, I know what you mean."

Alice blushes.

"Sorry, you thought I was hitting on you and now…"

Alice shakes her head and glances along the counter to see if the genius is coming back to save her anytime soon. "No," she says. "That's not it."

Will shrugs. His smile fades.

"*Shit*," Alice thinks. "*Now he's gonna think that I don't like him because he's gay.*"

"It's not ... it's just," Alice says. "My brother, the one you remind me of. Well, he's..."

Will nods. "Right," he says. "He's gay too, huh?"

Alice nods.

"So where you living Alice?"

"Thirty-Seven and Fifth," Alice says. "It's a work thing."

Will nods. "We're over on Avenue B. It's kind of cool over there, you know it?"

Alice shakes her head.

"You should come have a coffee sometime," Will says. "It's different. It's less ... well, less Fifth Avenue I guess."

The genius interrupts them. Alice thinks for a moment he has a glob of moisture hanging from his nose ring, but then she realises it's a chrome ball. She didn't notice it before.

"Here you go guys. Sorry about that. They're both from the same batch. Very rare, so sorry and all. Just go pick up two new ones and give this to the guy on the till." He hands them a slip of paper.

Outside the store, Will and Alice hesitate. "Hey sis... I'm thinking we should go to that coffee shop over there and check these out. In case they're also from the same batch."

Alice smiles. "Good thinking," she says.

Back in her apartment, Alice feels elated. *"I met someone,"* she thinks. *"I actually God darn met someone."*

She pulls the iPod box and Will's business card from her bag. Sure, he's gay, so he's not going to be anything but a friend. But that's almost better. A friend is more what she needs right now.

She props the card next to the phone. She'll wait a week before she calls him. So he doesn't think she's stalking him. And then she'll go over to Avenue B for coffee. She *will*.

She smiles to herself. He looks so like Michael. Lovely Michael. She looks at the phone, and then glances at the alarm clock. 13:55.

13:55 Eastern – makes ... she counts on her fingers. About six pm in Berlin. He'll be on his way home. She settles into the armchair and dials the number.

# The Stuff Of Dreams

Natasha rolls her eyes and sighs.

"So you can't even, like, *try* and feel a bit happy for me?" Fred asks, his intonation flat with sarcasm.

But Natasha can't; she doesn't trust his judgement. And in truth, Fred understands why – she has a point. He *did* meet the guy in *Lederhead*, after all. Natasha thinks relationships should read like Hallmark greetings cards. And Fred's life doesn't. It *really* doesn't!

Fred is one of only four people in *Lederhead*. One of them, Fred can't quite remember his name, Bernard, or Bertrand – something in the 'B's anyway – is the guy he went home with two weeks before. He berates himself for being here – again! He has promised himself he isn't going to do this anymore. But he isn't too hard on himself either. Fred knows his limits.

Between Fred and the B guy, there are two others. One is watching the porn video above the bar, he doesn't look well – his swollen belly and wasted cheeks clear giveaways of long-term antiviral medication.

But the other guy, the one nearest Fred is a stunner. Big built, a square, American, soap opera chin. He's wearing tight leather jeans – very like Fred's – and a skinny black *Rob*

T-shirt. His biceps – clearly pumped up with a little hormonal supplementation – look great bulging at the edges of his T-shirt.

Fred's dick stirs, and he becomes aware of the heavy cockring he is wearing. Of course it's all fantasyland, the guy is an untouchable – one of those beautiful, built, porn-star visions that you occasionally see but never actually get to have sex with. He's out of Fred's league. He's pretty much out of everyone's league.

Fred wonders what the guy is doing here at *Lederhead*. He's always surprised to see people like that sitting alone in a bar. You'd think that with those looks, he could have anyone; you'd think he'd have better things to do than sit in a bar alone on a Wednesday night.

Fred checks the guy in the mirror, scans the dark stubble of his chin, wonders how tall he is … one metre eighty, one metre eighty-five?

His dick stirs again, and he fidgets, then stands and heads across the bar towards the dungeon door. He's aware that everyone knows where he's going. He hopes that neither Mr B nor the sick guy will follow him.

He will tour the passages of the dungeons, and if there's no action there either, then he'll just go home. He's behind on his sleep anyway.

He wanders, beer in hand, along the arched tunnel. He glances to the right at the sling suspended from the ceiling. He remembers the last *Big Herr* party and his dick hardens. He hooks his thumb into the pocket of his jeans so that his hand rests on it as he walks.

He walks on and looks to the left. Two guys are kissing beside the wooden cross. He remembers being strapped there, fucked there at his first party... Jesus, the things he did with Richard! It had been dangerous – sure. Out of hand – wildly so. But, boy, what a hit! Compared to the ecstasy of being tied up, fucked in public, random hands all over him, well, no drug can compare.

He lightly caresses the front of his jeans and swigs again at his beer then moves on. No, it's dead tonight. No action, nothing, nada.

He reaches the end of the corridor, where the wooden stocks provide the final private shagging opportunities, where, during the big summer parties, he has seen a dick sticking out through every gap – almost surreal really.

He turns to head back and jumps. Right behind him against the wall, a man is standing, thumbs linked into waistband. Did he miss him in the dark or did he just appear?

Fred can't see his face, only the shine of his leathers. His dick stiffens anew and strains against the chrome.

He tries to walk nonchalantly past the guy, but he feels self-conscious. His footwork seems false, awkward; he fears he may be swaggering. But as he passes, the guy reaches out and brushes against his leg, so Fred turns. It's him. It's the untouchable, all one metre eighty-five of him. Fred swallows hard. The guy grins revealing perfect white teeth. "Well, *hello*," he says in English, his voice velvety with sex.

Fred swallows hard again and steps towards him. He looks even better – the half-light accentuates the angle of his jaw. He takes Fred's hand and pulls it against his crotch. His dick is hard and hot beneath the hide.

He starts to unbuckle Fred's belt. Fred runs his hands across the guy's chest – he can feel a harness beneath the T-shirt. "Ja," he says. "Ach, Jaaa!"

His jeans crumple to the floor, pulled downwards by the weight of his belt. His dick springs forward and upward struggling to lift the heavy piercing, like a miniature body-builder working out.

The guy takes a deep breath and slips a finger through the ring. "Oh yeah man," he says, his voice pure porn-star American. "Oh man…"

He pushes Fred to his knees, pulls Fred's face against his crotch. Fred breathes in the leather, pushes his nose and tongue through the gap, licks at the flesh and hair beyond.

He reaches up under the guy's T-shirt and grasps the straps of his harness.

"Oh man," the guy murmers. "You are the stuff of dreams."


So no, Natasha doesn't think it can work out. "I tell you Nat," Fred insists. "You'll see."

She rolls her eyes again and smiles weakly. "You're hopeless," she says.

Fred shrugs. "Why? Why is it hopeless, I mean just because we met…"

"In a sado-maso sex club," Natasha interrupts pointedly.

"It's a leather bar," Fred corrects her. "It's just a…"

"A leather bar where people tie each other to crosses, whip each other 'til they bleed, and get gang raped, right?" She raises an eyebrow. "A rose is a rose, Fred," she says.

Fred snorts.

Natasha frowns. "What?"

Fred shakes his head. "Never mind," he says. "You wouldn't understand. Anyway, it was just a bar; it was just a Wednesday night in a bar," he insists.

Natasha scoops the froth from her cappuccino and eats it. The coffee itself is still too hot to drink. "You told me you had sex with him in the bar, Fred," she says.

"Not sex exactly," Fred says, shrugging cutely.

Natasha leans forwards and looks him in the eye. "Don't get all Bill Clinton with me," she says. "You sucked him off, you both came; where I come from – or rather where *you* come from – that counts as sex."

Fred grins.

"And it's not big and it's not clever," Natasha admonishes.

Fred glances around the coffee shop in case anyone is listening, then looks back at Natasha and bites his lip. "It is actually," he says. "*Big,* that is."

Natasha blows through her lips and shakes her head. "Oh Fred," she says sadly.

*"What?"* Fred asks. "What is your problem?"

"Can't you see Fred? Can't you see how contradictory you are? Can't you see that the least likely place in the whole world for you to meet the man of your dreams is in a sex club?"

"Only I did," Fred says. "I *did* meet him in a sex club. And he *is* the man of my dreams."

"Maybe you need to change your dreams," Natasha says.

"Why?"

"Why? *Jesus!*" Natasha mutters. "Look, you met him in a sex club, and then you had sex with him in a sex club. And you've been having sex with him ever since. But it's just sex; it's just anonymous sex. End of story."

"Why do that?" he says. "Why curl up your lip and call it anonymous sex? You sound like some Christian…"

Natasha shrugs and composes the features of her face into a mockery of seriousness. "Did you know his name?" she asks. "When you first had sex?"

"So what?" Fred says. "I mean, what's so wrong with that? And I do now! So what?"

Natasha shakes her head. "Nothing, in *principle*," she says. "But dreaming about going on holidays together, wondering when his birthday is… Well, that's not healthy Fred, because it isn't going to happen. And you'll just be sad all over again."

Fred opens his mouth to speak and then closes it again without saying a word.

"And it's what you *always* do," Natasha points out.

"I dated Richard for nearly six months," Fred argues.

Natasha nods. "Yeah, if you can call being tied to a cross and gang raped *dating*."

"It *was* amazing though," Fred says.

"But *not* very classy," Natasha says.

"Sometimes I think you're just jealous," Fred says.

Natasha snorts and stares into the middle distance. She wonders how that would be. If straights could just wander into a bar and get a good shagging… If such places existed, would she go? And if not why not? But then, maybe they do.

Maybe she just doesn't know about them. Maybe she just doesn't *want* to know about them.

"It was, though..." Fred is saying. "Amazing, that is. You wouldn't understand, but it was *the* most amazing feeling."

Natasha pulls her focus back onto Fred's face. She has known him since secondary school. Dear, darling Fred. She turns and looks out of the window. A tram trundles down the street. She can see Fred so clearly. She can see his future all mapped out. And it's not good.

She looks at their reflection in the plate glass window, and for a moment Fred morphs into her sister; she actually sees her sister, orange hair and all, sitting there beside her. The vision is so convincing she shoots a sideways glance at Fred to check that he is still there. "That's what my sister used to say," she says quietly. "That it was so amazing, that I wouldn't understand."

Fred sighs heavily.

"Well, it *is*," Natasha says.

"That's not really fair," Fred says quietly. "Your sister was lovely. But she was a junky."

Natasha can't explain why. She can't find the words or even the concept to explain to Fred why it *is* the same. But it is. In some way it is *exactly* the same.

"You're right," she says after a while. "It is different. My sister really *couldn't* stop."

Fred reaches out and touches her hand across the table. "You still miss her lots huh?"

Natasha nods.

"But it gets easier right?"

Natasha nods again. "Yeah," she says. "I guess it does. But anyway…"

"But *anyway*. This is different. I've been seeing Max for *weeks*, just one on one … and you'll meet him soon. He's lovely. And hot."

"Only he lives with someone else," Natasha says pointedly.

Fred nods. "Yeah, but he promised me that he's going to leave him. I told you."

Natasha rolls her eyes again. It often seems to her like her gay friends are twenty years behind in their sexual maturity, as if they are having to do adolescence – first crushes and all – at thirty-five instead of fifteen.

"Fred, dear," she says. "Listen and learn – the married ones *don't* leave. They *never* leave. And the ones from out of town *always* make a mistake writing down the phone number. And the ones who are too broke to buy you a drink, are *always broke*. And the ones who fall in love at first … *suck…*" – here she nods at him seriously – "*always* get their hearts broken. Why can't you just find a nice, normal relationship?"

"Says the girl who's seeing a married, illegal immigrant Iraqi."

Natasha snorts. "Yeah, well…" she says.

# Too Late To Say

Max stands holding the phone. He hears the click on the line, but still he stands there, the handset pressed to his ear. He thinks of nothing at first, nothing at all. It's as if his mind has been anesthetised. He stares, his eyes not quite in focus, at the wall opposite.

After a while, the repetitive tone from the telephone exchange pierces his bubble – it starts to irritate him. He delicately replaces the handset on the base and glances over his shoulder – he has lost track of his position within the room. Seeing the armchair behind him, he lets his knees fold.

He pulls up his legs and wraps his arms around them and stares across the room at the Berlin skyline beyond the window. "*I didn't tell him*," he thinks.

He watches the clouds drifting from left to right, the shadows sweeping across the city. "*I didn't tell him,*" he thinks again.

The sky is blue and then grey, and then blue again. He watches how the light changes, how the blue fades, then starts to turn to pink.

He thinks of nothing at all; he feels nothing either. Only the single thought, *I didn't tell him*, followed occasionally by, *it's too late*, drifts through his mind.

He hears a church bell ringing and automatically, out of sheer habit, he counts the bells – seven pm. He was supposed to be gone by now; Michael was supposed to be home by now.

He realises that he hasn't eaten since breakfast, and wonders briefly if he is hungry. His stomach is so tight – so knotted – that it's hard to identify any specific feeling that *might* be hunger. And anyway, he has no food in. *Michael* has no food in – it was his turn to shop. And he was supposed to be gone by now. He was supposed to have told him.

In the street below, a car brakes, tyres screech, and Max's face twitches in expectation. The crash doesn't come, but an image of an impact, a vague, shadowy image of a body thrown aside, sweeps across his vision. He will never know exactly how it happened. He will probably never know more than he knows now, for officially of course, he is nothing to Michael. It's mere chance that he was still here when the police called. Yes he was supposed to be gone by now.

And now he will never be able to tell him. And he will never be able to *not* tell him.

Max wipes a hand across his mouth and shivers. He crosses the room and peers down at the street below. Red lights tail away to the right, white headlamps creep down the hill to the left.

He shivers again and shuts the window as a new, different version of how it happened – the second of many to come – pushes its way into his mind. This time it is accompanied by the subsonic thud of the impact. He blinks and turns back into the room.

He looks at all Michael's things. *So much stuff!* And it strikes him as absurd that all of these things, these CDs and pictures, all this bric-a-brac that describes so accurately, so specifically who Michael is – *was* – should continue to exist, even though the life they describe does not. He frowns. *How can that happen? How can someone be there, and then, just...*

There are probably things he should do – things that someone in his position should be doing, but he can't, for the moment, think what they might be.

Standing in the middle of the room in the fading light, it seems as if Michael's stuff is crowding him, it makes him feel vulnerable.

He pulls his eyes away from Michael's camera, filled with fresh photos of them both – fresh photos he hasn't even seen yet – and returns to the armchair and sits as before, staring through the window at the skyline beyond. After a while he starts to feel calmer again.

His mobile vibrates in his jeans, so he wriggles and writhes and pulls it free.

"Hello?" he says quietly, clearing his throat.

"Hi babe." Fred's voice is bright and optimistic, incongruous and absurd – a voice from another time, a voice from another life. "I just got in. Where are you?" he says.

Max clears his throat again. "I'm still here," he says, his voice a whisper.

"Where?" Fred asks. "*Where* are you?"

Max tries to say, "At Michael's," but his voice fails. He can't say the name. He coughs.

"You *bastard*," Fred says, slowly and with feeling. "You're still there, aren't you?"

Max swaps the phone from one trembling hand to the other.

"Fred, I…" he says.

"You promised," Fred says. "You *promised*. Today, you said."

"I … he's…" Max covers his mouth with his free hand.

Fred snorts. "And I believed you. I'm such a sucker. Did you even tell him?" Fred asks. "Did you even say *anything*? I bet you didn't even say anything, did you?"

Max shakes his head. "No," he says flatly. "I didn't tell him. I didn't tell him anything."

After a long silence, Fred says, his voice now level with restraint, "I'm sorry Max, but, but … I'm sick of this. If you're not going to…"

"I can't," Max says. "He's…"

"No," Fred says. "No, and the truth is, you don't *want* to, do you? You still love him. God! I am *such* a mug."

Max shakes his head. "Fred, you don't…"

"Enough," Fred says. "I *do* understand. And it's fine Max, really it is. You love him more than me, you always did. Look. I'm sorry, I've got to go."

Max pinches his nose and squeezes his eyes against the tears. He lowers the mobile to his lap and watches it until the screen dims.

"It's true," he says. "Oh God! It's true. And I didn't tell him."

# Slipping Through

Yasser places his hands between his knees and stares at the frosted glass door. He wonders if the house-of-cards that is his life is going to fall again. It's not that he can't rebuild it somehow, in fact, he has utter faith that he can, it's just that he built it as strong as he could. He's exhausted from doing everything he should, everything he can, only to see a fresh gust blow the whole damn thing over again.

It has been like this forever, or rather it's been completely different, yet in some way the same, as if this, this inability to build anything durable, to ever manage more than a single row of cards before a draught makes them topple, or someone walking by jogs the table, is a personal curse, built into the very fabric of his life.

Of course things here in Germany are different. Destiny is less predictable, or maybe it *is* just as predictable but at least there are gaps you can slip through from one destiny to another. In Iraq everything was mapped out. You knew where to live, where to work. Even what you should think was carefully defined. And that was fine as long as you did have somewhere to live, somewhere to work, something you were allowed to believe. But when the wind changed in

Iraq, there were no gaps to slip through. If the winds of change decided that your group, or race, or sometimes just you personally were non-grata, well, there were no walls to crouch behind.

But now Yasser lives in Berlin, and Saddam is gone, and who could be sad about that? The Germans are organised too – they pride themselves on it. But it's nothing compared to the Baathists. There are still gaps, and sometimes they are so slim you can't spot them until they are upon you, but Yasser hopes one will appear. Yasser is praying, is forcing himself to believe in a last minute reprieve.

And if it doesn't happen? If he truly loses his job? Well, the rest will probably crash to the ground.

His asylum status is already in doubt. The Merkel government no longer considers Iraq unsafe. I mean, do any of them *watch* the news? So, no, the Germans don't think there is any longer any reason why the likes of Yasser can't just go 'home'.

The fact that nearly every week someone he knows still dies is apparently neither here nor there, not now that Saddam is gone. And of course it is different. Destiny, once so organized, has become random; the Grim Reaper, once so methodical, now staggers around as if drunk.

So if Yasser loses his job, he will probably lose his case review. And if he loses his job he will lose his flat. And if he loses his case review he will lose Natasha.

Yes, it can all still come crashing down.

If only he hadn't been fiddling with change, or the guy hadn't lurched off the kerb, or it happened at a different time.

If he just had more than a week to find another job before the asylum interview...

But in a week, there's just no way. Especially with the majority of Berlin thinking he looks like a terrorist. How ironic! No, in a week, there's no chance. No chance at all.

He strokes his chin, now smoothly shaven, back how it was, how it had to be under Saddam. He snorts. Freedom! People here think they are so free. But try to get a job with olive skin and a full beard, try to flag a taxi in a Jallaba, and you'll see how free you are.

The door to the office opens, and Herr Reinhardt, the personnel manager, beckons him in. He can feel the breeze from the open window. He can see the trembling of the house of cards.

"Guten Tag," Reinhardt says stroking his moustache. "Wie geht's?"

Yasser replies that he's fine. He tries to read the paperwork on the desk, but German is hard enough, even when it's the right way up.

"A very unfortunate business," Reinhardt is saying, tapping the page and then wringing his hands. Yasser pays more attention to the gestures than the words. It's not that his German is poor; it's simply that people don't seem to say what they mean here. The gestures seem to be a better indicator of what is to come.

"... one accident too many..." Reinhardt is saying.

Yasser remembers sitting in front of the Baath party official the day he had to leave. He remembers him saying the same words – different place, different time, different language, but the same words. Destiny repeating itself, like a personal curse.

"But the autopsy showed that the impact was light, and though it provoked the haemorrhage, it wasn't actually the cause…"

Yasser has no idea what Reinhardt is talking about. There must be key words being used he doesn't know. He frowns and watches Reinhardt stroke his moustache, and thinks that it looks like Saddam's, and thinks that, well, he can get away with it because his skin is so pale, and thinks that maybe this – this attentive watching of people's gestures – is what it feels like to be deaf.

"… on the phone to a relative when the accident happened," Reinhardt says, "and you're really lucky, because she isn't pressing charges. She seems to think that it's *her* fault."

Yasser frowns and restrains a smile. *Lucky* he knows.

Reinhardt shrugs. "Aren't you happy?" he says.

Yasser smiles vaguely. "So is OK?" he says, raising an eyebrow.

Reinhardt nods. "Yes, you can go back to work on Monday."

Yasser covers his mouth with a sweaty palm. His eyesight blurs as tears well forth. He wants to hug Reinhardt; he wants to run and jump and dance for joy. He wants to buy Natasha something beautiful. "Thank you," he says with a nod of the head.

Reinhardt nods at him and stands. "Just be careful," he says.

Yasser nods and stands, clumsily knocking the chair over as he does so. "Very," he says, picking it up. "I will be so careful. You will not believe."

Yes, things are different here. The gaps in destiny just let you slip through. And that changes everything.

13:55 EASTERN STANDARD TIME

# A Bus In Berlin

As the line shuffles forward, Will says, "I didn't think you'd ever come, I mean, it's been months!"

Alice lifts a plastic flap and pulls the salad towards her, places it on her tray. "Yeah," she says. "It was a long time ago. Two months and three days," she adds, realising as she says it that this sounds weird.

*"It's still too soon,"* she thinks. *"God, I'm still not ready."*

"I'm sorry about that," she says. "It's just, you know, I've had a lot on."

Will nods and turns to order a sandwich – Mozzarella and sun-dried tomato on rye. Alice guesses that he doesn't really believe her – about being busy – and then decides that she doesn't really care.

"So what's new?" Will prompts as they slide into a booth.

Alice shrugs. "Not much," she says, putting her bag and magazine on the far side of the Formica table.

"But, if you've been busy..." Will prompts.

Alice frowns. *How to do this? How to do this whole getting to know someone thing without mentioning the elephant in the room?*

"I had to go away," she volunteers. "Family stuff."

Will nods. "Back to good ole Alabama?"

Alice shakes her head. "Berlin," she says, "actually."

Will nods, and coughs. He has decoded the vibe.

"OK..." he says pedantically.

"Yes," Alice says.

"Good sandwich. I love this place," Will says, trying unconvincingly to change the subject.

Alice nods. "I'm sorry Will. I'm not being secretive. It's just..."

Will nods. "Family stuff. It's OK."

Alice nods.

Will squints. "It's your brother who's in Berlin right? Do I remember that correctly?"

Alice nods slowly. She stares right through him.

"Well, good," Will says. "At least my memory is still working OK! Jude was telling me, just yesterday..."

"He's dead," Alice says flatly.

Will freezes, a slice of mozzarella hanging from his lip, then, as if the pause button has been released, he bites through it. "I'm sorry, I..." he says.

Alice shakes her head and sighs. "It's OK," she says. "How could you know? I should have phoned you before. But I was, you know, all over the place."

Will nods again. "I bet," he says. He fingers the edge of the magazine. "Do you want to talk about it, or..."

Alice snorts and smiles weakly. "You know," she says after a pause. "I do actually, only, I mean ... it seems kind of inappropriate."

Will shrugs. "It's life. Nothing's ever *inappropriate,* well, except dishonesty maybe."

Alice nods and sighs deeply. She forks a slice of tomato and thinks how much she hates plastic cutlery. "He was hit by a bus," she says. She laughs sadly. "It sounds absurd, doesn't it?"

Will nods thoughtfully. "A bus. In Berlin?"

Alice nods and swallows. She clears her throat. "Just the wing mirror actually. It … just clipped him on the back of the head."

Will blinks slowly and shakes his head.

"It was…" She shrugs. "It was nothing really – just a clip. But his…" She pauses to clear her throat. "His brain haemorrhaged … and he just … *died,*" she says, with a shrug.

Will reaches across the table and Alice lets him take her wrist. She looks up at him and realises her eyes are watering. "He was twenty-nine, Will. He was just twenty-nine."

Will squeezes her wrist and furrows his brow. "I'm so sorry Alice," he says. "These things just don't make any sense."

Alice pulls her hand free and pulls a tissue from her bag. "I don't know why I'm telling you this really," she says. "Only, well…" she glances up at him and smiles sadly. "You do look so like him, and," she shrugs, "and he died the day I met you, in the iPod store … which is weird." She covers her mouth.

Will runs a hand across his brow. He feels a little sick.

"I phoned him when I got home," Alice says. "That day? When I got home from the Apple store? He was fine. He

had just bought some flowers, for this guy he was seeing …
Max."

Will pinches the end of his nose. "Geeze Alice," he
says.

"And then," Alice shrugs. Her face crumples, and tears
start to flow freely.

Will's mouth drops. "You mean, you were actually
talking to him when…"

Alice nods, stands, and pushes clumsily from the stall.
"Sorry, I have to…" she mutters.

When Alice returns, she is visibly recomposed. "Sorry about
that," she says, over-brightly. "It just kinda hits me in waves."

Will nods and reaches for her hand but she pulls away.
"It'll just set me off again," she says. "Let's just talk about
something else, can we?"

Will nods and swallows. His own eyes are watering. "I
… erm…"

Alice straightens her back and slicks her hair. "So, you
still over on Avenue B, right?"

Will nods. "That's correct," he says.

They sit in silence for a moment. Will scans the room
for subject matter, before nodding at Alice's magazine on the
table. "You like Boyle?" he asks.

Alice frowns, so Will taps the cover of the magazine,
then spins it around, turning T.C. Boyle's face towards her.

"Oh, no … to be honest I never read anything by him.
You?"

Will shrugs. "I read something years ago. *East is East*
or something. But Jude – my partner – he worships him."

Alice nods.

"He's a budding writer," Will tells her with a smile and a shrug. "I think he's really good. But he lacks, you know, confidence."

Alice nods. "What does he write? I only really read shorts ... and poetry, so I probably never..."

Will shrugs. "Oh he's hardly had anything published. It's just a hobby, mainly short stories and stuff. He loves Boyle, though."

Alice pushes the magazine across the table.

"Take it," she says. "There's a big piece on Boyle in there. And I'm pretty much done with it now."

Will raises an eyebrow. "Yeah?" he says. "If you're sure. Otherwise I'll just tell him, he'll buy his own cop..."

Alice shakes her head and gives the magazine another push. "Please," she says.

13:55 EASTERN STANDARD TIME

# Woodpile

Jude sips at his mug of cocoa and taps his thumb rhythmically against the glossy page of the magazine. He stares at the flickering image on the TV screen; a shiny presenter – with perfect hair and a perfectly knotted tie – is moving his lips rapidly, smiling cutely.

Jude feels suddenly weary, unexpectedly hollow, empty and alone. He frowns. *"And where did that feeling come from?"* he wonders.

For it is absurd. A moment ago – what, five minutes? – he was feeling blissfully contented, was counting his blessings for the apartment, for his job, for the love of his life... He stops to consider this value judgement, confirms it as correct, and then continues. Yes, he has it all, a great apartment, perfect health, a positive bank balance, and the *love of his life*, asleep next door in the bedroom. So why the sudden emptiness?

He raises a hand and strokes his beard and thinks of his friend Jemma, his oldest closest, share-everything friend. She once told him that he would never be happy, that it was in his genes to be dissatisfied. She said, "If you ever stop complaining, I'll be worried; if you ever stop complaining, I'll know you're dead."

He smiles at the thought and chews the inside of his mouth. So is that the explanation? Is this sudden gnawing, this, *is-that-all* feeling, simply Jude being Jude?

He sips his cocoa again and looks down at the magazine on his lap, at the shine of the paper, at the reflection of the red standard lamp right down the middle of T.C. Boyle's head. – *Such a strange looking chap! Jealousy maybe?*

He tries to trace the origin, for this thought, this feeling has descended upon him like the sudden chill when a cloud unexpectedly passes in front of the winter sun.

*Winter.* Winter is coming.

So is it jealousy? Is he just feeling jealous at T.C. Boyle's commercial success, when his own manuscripts sit unpublished in a box, or at Boyle's apparent contentedness? At his literary cleverness? Jude shakes his head, sighs, puts the magazine down, then crosses the room and stares at the street below.

The air is cooler over here; he can sense that it is colder outside this evening. He fiddles with the catch and slides the window open, letting a blast of chilled air and traffic noise into the room, and then, just as quickly, he closes it again. The hustle and bustle of New York – it just never stops.

He tours the room, switching off the silent TV and then, one by one, the three lamps, before heading through to the bedroom. He can hear Will snoring beyond the flimsy panelling of the door.

With a frown, he turns and pads back through to the lounge, where he switches on a single reading light, sits and re-opens the magazine.

He stares at T.C. Boyle for a moment, at his orange nest of hair, at the, what? *madness?* in his eyes, and then, slowly, self consciously, he re-reads the article; for the secret lies there. Some thought, some *thing* that he didn't notice has made him feel quite strange, quite profoundly sad in fact.

He reads about T.C. Boyle's tenure, about the adventures of his recent author tour, his home life, his daily routine, his preparations for winter ... *there!*

"... *and in the afternoons I like to do something physical, at the moment, for instance, we're working on the woodpile, getting it ready for winter.*"

He feels it, the tug on the heartstrings, the plucking at something ... at what? What is it?

The chill. The emptiness. The woodpile.

It's bigger than him, vast in fact; some weird profound tapping-in that he doesn't understand.

Something ... *elemental* is missing from his life. And it's there, in that phrase. *Getting the woodpile ready for winter.*

It's *all* in there. Everything that is wrong with his life is contained in that phrase; everything that is missing from this perfect city life, from this successful career, from this cosy relationship, from this temperature-controlled apartment. For winter is coming. And who would know it?

He wants to cut wood. He *needs* to cut wood. He snorts and shakes his head. He has never cut wood in his life. He's a city boy, born and bred. And yet there's a hole in the very depths of his being – a great chasm of yearning. And it's not from his life; it's not from his own memories at all.

Transmission by popular culture possibly – he's seen enough films of people living off the land to know ... but he can *smell* the damp wood. He knows the *texture* of the tree-bark in his hands. Genetics then? Could the need to touch the soil, to smell the pinesap, the aching need to ... *get ready! Winter's coming!* Could that be genetics? Could that stuff really be coded in his DNA? Or is Jung right. Is it the collective consciousness of ancestors calling to him through the ages?

He re-reads the phrase again. "We're working on the woodpile, getting it ready for winter." He can feel the smooth shaft of the axe in his hand. He can see his breath rising as the temperature drops, as the sun fades behind the mountains. The hairs on the back of his neck bristle.

He switches off the light again and creeps through to the bedroom; shucks his jeans and T-shirt and slips as smoothly as he can beneath the light blanket. Will half wakes and rolls over.

"You OK?" he asks, in an otherworldly voice of sleep.

"I want to move to the country," Jude says quietly. "I want a stove and a garden, I want to grow vegetables. I want to chop wood for winter."

Will makes a grunting, *Mmmm* sound. "Sure," he says.

Jude lies on his back and stares at the ceiling and smiles. Will is snoring again, but beyond that, Jude can hear the trees swaying outside. He can feel the heavy quilt pressing down on him, the cold freshness of the air entering his nostrils. He snuggles to Will's back, protection against the beasts of the night and the icy winter.

# Still Scared

David presses his nose up against the window and has a sudden flashback to the bus he used to take to school. It was a double-decker, and he used to sit upstairs, always upstairs, preferably over the driver.

He hasn't been on a bus for years, not since his college years in fact. It's actually quite fun – a trip down memory lane. He remembers how upstairs was smoking, how the air was thick and grey; he remembers the feel of the bristly carpet material that covered the seats. He glances at his watch. And the bus is slow of course, only he didn't have a choice anyway. The car failed to start – an omen? A warning? Or just the perfect excuse to cancel. Only he didn't cancel. It's taken him a month to pluck up the courage, a month thinking about that poor American woman on the plane, flying home from her brother's funeral. A month thinking about mortality, about the fact that his own brother – or indeed, he himself – could die, and that they wouldn't have seen each other, wouldn't have *spoken* to each other for ten years. So no, he didn't cancel.

As the countryside gives way to the outskirts of Belfast, David tries to remember exactly how long ago it was. Ten years? Eleven?

Whatever the date, the event is as vivid as if it were yesterday – he can still remember every detail. Or is it a fusion he's remembering – all of the arguments, all of the drunken Christmases, the tense birthdays, all of the unspoken jealousies that led up to that moment, a sort of family archetype of conflict?

The bus swings into a depot – cold grey concrete poured in the Seventies, when cold grey concrete, swathes of it, was, for some reason, the future.

Three passengers alight, and three more mount – a sort of passenger exchange – and the bus swings back out onto the road.

Of course the last time they saw each other it was different from all the others, it was worse. Was it the fact that the abuse on that occasion had been aimed at Grace, his wife, that changed everything? The need to protect – the responsibility to say what had to be said on behalf of Grace who clearly couldn't defend herself against her brother in law? Or was it the same as ever, just one time too many, the straw that broke the camel's back, as their father used to say. Rather than an event, was it not just the culmination of a whole lifelong process of alienation?

He's feeling stressed, so he forces a deep breath and rolls his head around to stretch his neck muscles. But people change right? Their mother has told him that Colin's drinking is better. Yes, "better," she said – whatever that means.

He crosses his eyes and shakes his head.

But he's an adult now, he reminds himself. He's no longer the little brother. He's nearly fifty. He can defend himself. He can say what he wants. And he can get up and just walk away if it all goes wrong.

"*Ridiculous!*" he thinks. "*Feeling scared at fifty!*" But his palms are sweating and his stomach feels knotted all the same.

Yes, he can get up and walk away at any time. He can be honest and straightforward and if Colin starts any trouble he will clearly say that he objects, and, if necessary, walk away. That, as a grown man, is his inalienable right.

The bus takes forever, and as they pass Lisburn, memories flood his brain, memories of fights and beatings, of troops and hard times. The weather may be the same in Bangor, but at least they have the sea to look at, they have the endless sky.

Just outside Dungannon, he alights at the bus stop and walks the further hundred yards to the house. He knows exactly which one it is, even though they only bought it – were *given* it – six years ago. But he has driven past twice. Once before they moved in – just to fully appreciate the unfairness of his father's gesture. And once, just a week ago – to try to put a finger on his true feelings.

On the doorstep outside the bungalow, he almost changes his mind. At the final moment, standing on the welcome mat, sensing the interior, glimpsing movement beyond the patterned glass door, his hand falters as he reaches for the doorknob. The muscles he would use to turn away actually start to engage. But then the door opens and it's too late.

* * *

David shakes his head gently. "No really, I'm not drinking at the moment – doctor's orders." It's a lie of course, so he has already slipped into playing *The Game*. Younger brother searches for older brother's approval by trying to be cool, or at least, by providing a valid excuse – a doctor's note! – for *not* being cool.

"Actually I never drink during the day anyway," he adds. "It makes me sleepy."

It's a vague stab at honesty, a wimp's bash at freedom, liberation, adulthood.

The real reason he doesn't want to drink is so that he can keep a clear head. So that he can know what to say, what not to say – so that, if necessary, he can know exactly when to walk away.

"Well, aren't we the pious one," his brother says.

Yes, this is why David wants to stay sober. He wants to try to decode these phrases that slip from his brother's lips. He wants to understand, once and for all what they mean, what lurks in the depths of his brother's psyche that he could be affronted by a simple refusal to drink whiskey before lunch.

"They're starting on the veranda next month," Shannon, Colin's wife says, noticeably changing the subject.

David looks into her eyes and she holds his gaze a moment too long. A warning? A yearning? *Something* passes between them.

David frowns. Yes, maybe yearning ... longing. *Regret?*

*"Is this all there is?"* her eyes are saying. No, even that's not it. It's, this *is* all there is. *Don't fuck it up.*

David feels suddenly exhausted. He knows the visit is hopeless.

"It's costing twenty grand," Colin says, always a one to put the price on things.

David nods. "Twenty! The business must be doing well," he says.

Colin sighs and slops a refill into his glass. "The business, the business! You're well out of the business. No, we had to use the money that Dad gave us. We were saving it for a rainy day, and then we thought we'd use it – have somewhere to sit on a rainy day instead!"

The twenty thousand that Dad gave them then. David didn't know about that. He swallows; he isn't surprised. Colin was always the favourite – clearly undeniably, outrageously so. He got the business, a car, this house – a wedding gift... So David isn't surprised that there was an extra twenty grand; it's an old, old wound. Knowing it just twists the knife a little more.

"It's not going to be like the one Jim had though," Shannon says. "It's going to be one of those modern ones, all glass and wood. Col, show him the brochure."

"Triple glazed," Colin says, reaching for a catalogue on the coffee table.

David blinks and sits up straight. Not, in truth, to reach out for the proffered catalogue, but to get a closer look at his brother.

*"He's becoming our father,"* David thinks. *"He is our father."*

For their childhood home, a red brick bungalow almost identical to this one – not fifteen miles away from this point – had a sunroom too; Jim built it himself. The colour scheme here, the pale green and the beige woodwork, is exactly the colour of their childhood lounge. Even some of the furniture came from Dad's house – Colin had helped himself even before the funeral.

Colin is talking about the redevelopment of the shopping centre. "Still, I don't suppose you Bangor types get over here very often," he says.

In a revelatory moment, David suddenly sees his father's generosity for the trap that it truly is. He smiles. For years he has thought, *known*, he was hard done by. For years he has fought feelings of jealousy over the constant gifts, the never-ending handouts his brother received. But in this second it has all changed. It is *Colin* who is jealous. It is Colin who is trapped. And he never knew!

For David is the one who got away. He is the one who got to build his own life, exactly as he wanted it. All poor Colin could do was trundle down the track old Jim Stewart had laid before him.

"Not a lot, no," he says. "Only to see family." Here he winks at his brother.

Colin raises an eyebrow. "Yeah, well, it's not like you do that much," he says.

*"I can get up and walk away at any moment,"* David reminds himself.

Shannon catches David's eye. Her eyes again are deep with meaning. Is she imploring him not to rise to the bait, or begging him not to walk out?

"Shall I go serve up the dinner?" she asks, deftly sweeping the whiskey bottle from the coffee table as she stands. "I'm half starved."

Colin grabs the bottle by the base and puts it back on the table. "Away on, woman!" he exclaims. "I haven't finished with the Jameson."

*Away on!* It's exactly what their father used to say.

And there's more. This feeling of imminent danger, the slow wobbling out of control; the voice, slightly louder than need be, the redness in the cheeks… It's all hauntingly familiar too. The hairs on the back of David's neck prickle. The desire to run, the feeling of imminent danger is overpowering, but there is something happening here. He is on the verge of understanding something.

*His father* – sometimes so gentle, sometimes so understanding, and then suddenly so terrifyingly unpredictable, suddenly losing it, over nothing, over anything. And it always ended in violence of some kind – a slap, a punch, sometimes worse.

*Of course! It was the drink!* How could he not have realised? And that's why he wants to run now; that's why he's feeling scared. That's why he is whipped back into childhood every time his brother has a whiskey too many.

"What are you staring at?" Colin asks. "Lost your tongue, have you?"

David shakes his head. "Sorry," he says. "I was miles away." He turns to Shannon. "Yes, dinner would be great," he says. "I'm starved too."

13:55 EASTERN STANDARD TIME

# The Test That Broke The Camel's Back

S cott knew that Terry was a tester. He had submitted to – and passed – Terry's endless tests. He had passed hundreds since the beginning of their relationship three years ago.

To start with, the tests had been simple, barely coded, easily interpreted, and, for the most part, quickly dealt with.

There was the, 'If I don't call, will *he* call *me?'* test. Irritating, but in the end, not that hard to work around, especially with free weekend phone calls.

Later came, 'If I cause a big argument about nothing – about anything – just before the weekend, will he still spend it with me?' Scott found two ways to pass this. One was to just turn up on Friday night as if nothing had happened, and the other was not to turn up all weekend, but to turn up the following weekend as if nothing had happened. The latter solution – he felt – combining passing the test with light punishment for bad behaviour, seemed pretty perfect really.

But slowly the tests got harder to pass, more difficult to bear. Some of them, like the 'Oh no, sorry, I forgot to buy you a Christmas gift' test seemed more like an excuse for being mean than a test, *per se*. And though he felt he had failed this one – by stomping and crashing around the apartment all over the holidays, it seemed, when January came, that he had somehow passed after all by simply still being there.

The most popular test of the final year was the sulking, sighing, test. Hours spent on the phone listening to Terry complain about his job, about his social life, or simply saying nothing, managing to express misery through silence. The test, it seemed, was to try to force Scott to fail by hanging up. Sometimes he passed, and sometimes he failed. But it left a sludgy trail. The passage of the test was somehow destructive, and, as the same test trundled through the ragged ruts left by its previous and repeated passage, Scott found it harder and harder to put up with.

And the silent, sighing phone call test just kept on repeating. He presumed it was because he never found out quite how to pass it correctly. He tried the *pull yourself together* speech, and the *poor baby* dialogue. He tried saying, "I'm sorry, but I'm busy, and I really have to go." And finally he tried listening, numbly, for hours, until Terry eventually hung up, which, he would have guessed was the aim of the game. But somehow, even then, the sigh that Terry gave when he finally ended the conversation let Scott know that he had failed this one yet again. And so it kept coming.

Terry applied specific tests at all major milestones of the relationship. It sometimes seemed to Scott that Terry needed so strongly to be reassured that his relationship was solid that he, more often than not, appeared determined to break it.

When Scott organised the best birthday treat Terry had ever had, Terry became drunk and randomly abusive in the middle of the restaurant. The whole weekend was wrecked, just, Scott felt sure, to see if they could get through it.

And when Scott tried to integrate Terry into his deepest, longest held, most important friendships, Terry, at first, pretended he didn't much like Scott's friends, thus making Scott choose.

But Scott passed all of the tests with flying colours, because, in the end, no matter what Terry threw at him, Scott was still there come Monday morning. Terry, it seemed, felt almost reassured. *Almost.*

When Scott found a house for them to buy – a place where they could maybe one day live together, a beautiful log cabin up in the Pocono Mountains, which by an incredible stroke of luck they could actually afford – Terry knew he was getting into a serious commitment zone. It seemed he needed an ultimate test.

Terry went out on a weeknight. He got drunk enough to be weak on the details. He had (probably) unsafe sex with a (possibly) random guy in an unspecified bar. He knew he should tell Scott, for that was the point. But when it came to it, he just couldn't bring himself to hurt him that much. He did love him after all.

But the day they decided to buy the cabin; the day they decided how much to offer on the property; the day they sat and calculated how much to borrow and where from, how much to pay for it, well, Terry knew he had to tell Scott the truth. He knew he had to tell Scott everything. Faced with such a big commitment, Terry had to find out if their relationship was strong enough to bear what he had done.

And on any normal day, Scott would probably have passed that test too. Scott knew about gay relationships, and understood the male sex drive. He knew all about drunken attraction. The unsafe bit of it was harder, for it made Scott worry for his health, and it made him lose some respect for his partner.

And the fact that it was months ago made him worry about his partner's ability to lie to him, his capacity for hiding the truth, for cuddling up while not mentioning it. So Scott worried about the deceit.

But on any normal day Scott would have managed to grapple and understand all of these things – he would probably have passed this ultimate test with flying colours.

But today wasn't a normal day. Today was the day he had decided to buy a house with Terry. Today was the day he had decided to own a home with Terry.

And though he didn't really understand why, he found, the next morning, on waking, that he just didn't want to do that anymore.

Scott didn't feel guilty about ending the relationship, even though Terry wept and protested. He felt sad and lonely, but also liberated, also liberat*ing*. It was as if this was maybe what he was meant to do *all along*. It was as if this was maybe how Terry had always *wanted* him to pass the tests.

When Scott told a friend who had studied psychology about it all, she agreed, saying that in her opinion the tests weren't tests at all. In fact, she said, they had been attempts at sabotage, subconscious efforts to force Scott to smash up what Terry didn't dare smash up himself – an unsatisfactory relationship. And that seemed true. Because though Terry seemed less *unhappy* with Scott than without him, Scott had to admit that he had never seemed completely happy either. And then Scott did feel guilty. He felt guilty for having dragged them both through it all for so long.

13:55 EASTERN STANDARD TIME

# Like God

Will stands, a little shell-shocked from the drive, and stares reverentially at the cabin.

"I can hardly believe it," Jude says, his breath rising in the late morning sun like steam from a cartoon steam engine.

"No," Will agrees, sliding an arm around Jude's waist and pulling him close.

For it started as a whim, in fact, who knows *how* it started. But one morning Jude's waking words were, "I want a place in the country," and then, now, two years later, here they are. And strangely it hasn't been so hard either. Not yet anyway.

In the beginning, Will thought it was just another whim, just the latest, in fact, of Jude's many whims.

The cupboard in the hall – it houses a mountain bike, an ab-stretcher, a weird electrical body-building-cum-torture device, a pair of unused season tickets to the opera... That cupboard holds so *many* of Jude's past fads – Will even *calls* it the whim cupboard.

But *this* idea, this mad, almost unimaginably impractical, "I want a place in the country," idea *didn't* go away and somehow, without the two men ever really realising, through Internet searches and weekends away checking out this dreary tumbledown, or that termite ridden shack in red-neck land, through calls to realtors, and cutbacks to save money, through talking to friends who were looking too, but then changed their plans, through a pile of books about off-grid living and a night class in electrical wiring … well, it happened. Maybe the idea was just too big to fit in the whim cupboard. Anyway, here they are, side by side. "It's beautiful," Will says. "And the view! It's even better now than when we came before."

"Autumn," Jude says, looking out over the reds and ochres of the forest below, then scanning the horizon, and finally letting his sight rest upon the chunky logs of the cabin. "Now the real work begins," he says.

Will reaches behind him and pulls a sweater from the seat of the van. "Let's have lunch, and just enjoy this moment first though. This will never happen again, you know?"

Jude pecks him on the cheek. "OK, just half an hour though. I need to get all those batteries wired together, and the PV panels too. If I don't get the icebox up and running we'll have nothing to eat."

Will nods. "I know," he says. "We'll have lunch, and then we'll do exactly like we planned."

They sit side by side on the rotten wooden porch and pull the picnic – vacuum packed cheese and perfect industrial tomatoes, food suddenly out of phase with the rugged surroundings – from the bag.

"Do you think you can fix this?" Jude asks, rapping the step.

Will nods. "Wood holds no mysteries for me. But don't ask me to help you with the electricals. They are entirely your responsibility."

Jude grins and raises an eyebrow. "I know," he says. "Don't worry. It's all in hand."

Will laughs and looks out at the horizon again. Something miraculous has happened to Jude too. The city boy who wouldn't change a fuse has twelve thousand dollars worth of photovoltaic panels and deep discharge batteries filling the van, and is – or so he claims – about to connect them all together to make free grid quality 110v electricity.

"Are you scared?" Jude asks as he hands Will a beer.

"Scared? About your electricals?" Will laughs.

Jude shakes his head and bites into his sandwich. "Nah, about this whole thing. *Asshole!*"

Will shrugs and thinks about it. "I was feeling ... nervous, I guess you'd say. I was feeling worried, mainly that we'd get here and hate it, and have wasted all this time and money on a whim."

Jude nods. "Yeah, I thought that too."

"But now..." Will raises his eyebrows and nods out over the horizon. "I look at that view, and I breathe this air, and what I'm suddenly scared of is going back."

Jude blinks very slowly and leans into Will's side. "Hey, whatever happens, I mean, however it works out, it'll be fine, OK?"

Will nods. "I know," he says.

By the time the daylight fails, the sun crashing through the horizon in a blood-streaked car-accident of a sunset, the men are shattered.

Will has plugged the gaps in the walls with heavy tar-tape and lumps of hardboard, and has unwrapped the new mattress and dumped it onto the sagging springs of the rusting bed. The freezer is somehow humming beyond the window, and Jude's panels are lined up along the side of the house waiting for the morning sun.

"It's so cold," Jude says, hopping out of his jeans and diving under the quilt. "I mean, I knew it was cooler up here, but I didn't expect…"

"Yeah, we have to get the stove sorted tomorrow," Will says. "It shouldn't be too hard, I just need to replace those rusted conduits. And you're up on the roof anyway tomorrow, right?"

Jude nods. "Yep, if everything works then I'll try to get them all permanently mounted on the roof tomorrow."

Will snuggles against his side. "So we can have music?"

"Music, light, microwave," Jude giggles. "Anything you want babe."

Will shakes his head. "You amaze me sometimes," he says.

Jude grins. "I know," he says. "It's funny how easy things are in the end, when you just do them, you know, one step at a time."

Will yawns deeply. "God I'm so tired though. My eyes are going, you know, kinda cloudy from tiredness."

Jude nods. "Me too," he says, leaning over and blowing out the candle. "It's the driving."

"And the mountain air."

"Yeah, that does something too," Jude agrees.

The light of the half moon drifts through a gap in the curtains – actually they're towels – which Will has hung over the lone window.

Will snuggles against Jude's side for a few minutes, then snores once, and rolls away. Jude lies, sleepy yet awake, staring at the ceiling and listening to the sounds of the forest.

He feels like he has been here before – he feels like he has been exactly here once before – and he wonders if he dreamt it, or if he dreamt of the future, dreamt of this moment, or if he remembers it from a previous life, or if he just imagined it and then somehow made it happen.

As he starts to doze, his mind drifts; his thinking becomes vague and fluid.

So he thought it and that was enough to make it happen? Is that what he believes? But that would be a miracle, wouldn't it? If man had the ability just to imagine a situation and make it manifest, then man would be like God, wouldn't he? Man would *be* God, wouldn't he?

He smiles. He can hear the trees swaying outside. He can feel the heavy quilt pressing down on him, the cold freshness of the air entering his nostrils. He snuggles against Will's warm back.

13:55 EASTERN STANDARD TIME

.

# Part Two

*"Never idealise others.*
*They will never live up to your expectations."*

**– Leo F. Buscaglia**

13:55 EASTERN STANDARD TIME

# A Really Good Decision

Simon says, "Wow!" The door to the apartment is still open behind him.

"Cool huh?" Hannah replies, grinning lopsidedly. The lopsided grin is a new thing – one of many new things about Hannah he is managing to ignore.

She is standing, hands on hips, in front of an enormous plate-glass window.

"It's, erm, big," Simon says. "It's *really* big."

Hannah nods knowingly, then spins to face the window. "And look at the view," she says.

Simon doesn't move. He remains in the doorway. In truth his brain is having trouble taking it all in. The sheer scale of the place, the very idea that she, they...

"You like it though, right?" Hannah says, lobbing the words over her shoulder at him.

Ever since college, Simon and Hannah have struggled; actually, if truth be told, *he* even struggled *through* college, but since college, well, it just hasn't stopped.

They have struggled finding jobs, keeping jobs. They have struggled to find time to see each other when the jobs that they *had* found were at opposite ends of the country. But above all, they have struggled with accommodation issues.

In the last three years, since they have been working in London, they have lived in four short-let apartments – cheap fill-in deals between tenants (too temporary to be satisfying), and three groggy bed-sits (too many cockroaches). They have lived in holidaying friends' apartments (with and without authorisation), and have had numerous stays in the miniscule rooms of a cheap hotel.

It's a ridiculous state of affairs for two graduates in their mid twenties, but there you go – London real estate is outrageously expensive. So the idea, the very concept that they might move to this barn-like loft apartment – well – it blows Simon's mind.

"Simon, tell me you like it," Hannah repeats, spinning back towards him on the heel of a boot.

The spinning and the boots are new things too. She used to wear plimsols. She was famous for her huge range of coloured plimsols. He liked them. Simon freezes his mind so as not to think about the new Hannah. He doesn't know why he does this *freeze* thing with Hannah – he would only know the *why* if he *didn't* freeze his thoughts, if he let his mind travel to the end of that road, but there lie demons.

He used to do the same thing when his parents were arguing. To start with he used to sing songs in his head to avoid thinking about whatever it was tempting but dangerous to contemplate. But nowadays he can just flick a mental switch, and with a puff of imaginary dry ice, the thought is frozen in its tracks. It doesn't change the outcome of course, any more than it prevented his parents separating, but it makes the waiting easier.

"Of course I like it," he says. "I *really* like it." He pronounces really, *w*eally. He has always had trouble with his 'R's. In a way it's laziness – he knows that. For if he concentrates really hard on the shape of his mouth he can manage a pretty good approximation of the correct sound for 'R', but it slows him down, and so, he decided years ago that it was better to say *weally* and *wising* than to sound permanently thick. "But I mean," he continues. "How are we going to pay for it? I mean, how much *is* this place? How much are the *w*epayments going to be?"

Hannah crosses the room, in her clip, clip, clipping boots, and closes the front door behind him. "The *Off The Grid* contract will cover it babe. I told you," she says.

Simon frowns. The "babe" appellation is new too. *Freeze.* "And what about after that?" he asks. "What do we do then?"

Hannah gives him a gentle push into the room. "Well, look around then!" she says, then, answering his question, "and I would hope that at some point in the future you can contribute something too."

Simon walks across the gleaming floor and stands in front of the wall of glass. Beyond it the London skyline is stunning. The daylight is starting to fade and even as he watches, the spotlights on the Tate Modern light up.

"It's like something f*w*om a TV programme," Simon says. "Or like one of those images they show behind the news-*w*eaders."

Hannah moves to his side. "It doesn't look like anything from *my* TV programmes," she laughs.

Simon stares at the Tate, at the huge chimneys, and in his mind's eye he sees the smoke billowing from the power station that the building once was. He's thinking about the fact that Hannah's tiny TV production company, specialized as it is in programmes about downsizing, green living, and the big hit which has brought them to this point, *Off The Grid*, well, he's thinking about how ironic it is that the profits of that are going to pay for all this glass and chrome – for such a consequential *upsize*.

"You know, I'll never be able to afford a place like this," Simon says. "My wages probably won't pay the heating bill."

Hannah tutts. She never used to tutt either. *Freeze.*

"Simon, you have to stop being so negative," she says. "You won't be earning peanuts forever. I mean, I believe in you, and, well, you have to believe in yourself."

Simon frowns. "I *do* believe in myself," he says. "And I *don't* earn peanuts. I earned nearly three thousand last month. I just think that this place is beyond my ... beyond *our* means."

He pads across to the kitchen and stands in the doorway looking in. The kitchen alone is bigger than their current place. "It looks like an operating theatre," he says, shaking his head in awe at the gleaming steel surfaces.

He hears Hannah sigh behind him, and realises she's losing patience, so to placate her, he offers, "*Beautiful* though!" He looks back at her and she rolls her eyes and blows though her lips.

"Finally," she says. "Trust you to like the kitchen though. Come look at the bedroom!"

He crosses the lounge again and follows her up the wooden staircase to the mezzanine. "Wow," he says, leaning beside her on the guardrail and looking again at the view. The sky is almost dark now and the city sparkles before them. "If anyone out there has binoculars," he laughs.

"Ya," Hannah says.

The *ya* is new too. *Freeze.* "I thought we could put a row of those white roller blinds along here," she continues, tracing an imaginary line along the ceiling. "To let the light through but give us some privacy."

"I'm not sure," Simon says.

Hannah returns to his side. "Well, it's of no importance really," she says. "As long as we come up with some way to..."

"No, I mean about the apartment," Simon interrupts. "About this place."

"Jesus!" Hannah whispers. "What's wrong with you lately?"

He shrugs. "I'm not sure it's *us*," he says. "It's a *w*ich people's apartment."

"Well maybe we're *w*ich now," Hannah says. "Maybe you need to get used to that."

Simon winces. He hates it when people copy his 'R' thing. It actually makes him quite angry. He has challenged her about it a couple of times recently, and she says it's an accident. Automatic mimicry, she claims. But it only happens when she's angry. *Freeze.*

"*I'm* not," he points out, then with care, "*I'm* not ... r-ich."

"Then let me pay for it," Hannah says, her voice softening. "Let me do this for us."

"But then it'll be yours," he argues. "It'll be your apartment."

Hannah shrugs. "What does it matter?"

"And what about our values? What about g-r-een living and downsizing, and ecology…"

"Fuck principles," Hannah says. "I've been living with a family of cockroaches for months. Jesus, we spent last Christmas in an Easy Hotel. Do you remember that? Not a white Christmas, but an orange one. And now we can buy this, and we can be secure. It will be ours."

"*Yours,*" he counters quietly.

"OK, mine. So what? At least we'll be secure. At least we won't be at the whim of some landlord who…"

"Hey," Simon says, stroking Hannah's back. "I'm just saying that I don't see why it has to be so big, so showy."

"Simon, things change. People change. And what I need right now is an apartment that looks like me. That looks like a successful TV producer. When the people from Channel Four come over, or the Yanks from the Discovery Channel…"

"And what if you don't *get* another big cont-r-act?" Simon says. "How secure will we be then?"

"Oh, we'll get it. He's being greedy, that's all. He's asking for like, three times what we paid him for the first series, but he'll cave in eventually. Authors always do. They don't have a choice."

Simon wrinkles his brow. "But I thought you said he was underpaid," he says. "I thought you said you only paid him ten grand for the whole first…"

Hannah shrugs. "Yeah, but it's all a game isn't it. It's not the money; it's just, you know, the principle of it. No-one's gonna hold me to ransom. Especially not some one-hit author."

"A one-hit author who has made you pretty *w*ich," Simon says.

"Nah, he didn't make me *w*ich babe," Hannah says. "I did that all myself. Anyway, come on," she glances at her watch. "It's decision time. What's it going to be? Are we moving here, or are you staying in that dingy bed-sit?"

Simon frowns. He thinks about her words. Are *we* moving in here, or are *you* staying there. *Freeze.* He frowns.

Hannah tips her head from side to side cutely, as if peering through a dirty window. Simon stares at her impassively. Then slowly, he lets his brain thaw. He doesn't know why he does it now, at this particular instant, but he does, he switches off the ice. The melting of the icecaps; the terror of the flood; the joy of survival. And floodwater rushes through – *electrifying.*

"Hello?" Hannah prompts. She taps the toe of her boot. "Anyone home?"

Simon nods slowly, his eyes fixing hers almost madly. His brain is freewheeling. He feels eleven again, free and reckless. Tap. Tap. Tap. Hannah's boot beats out rhythm on the parquet.

He tilts his head slightly, then straightens and says, "Yes."

Hannah smiles contentedly, pecks him on the lips and spins towards the door. "Good decision," she says. "A *weally* good decision."

"Yes," Simon says again, stealing a final glance at the view – it is dark outside now and even more beautiful than before. "Yes, I'll be staying in my dingy bed-sit. You can move."

# Yanks And Paddies

An Irish guy at the end of the bar is raising hell about the name of the place – Paddy's. He's saying that it's an insult, a racist slur.

Scott fingers his pint and watches the bubbles break free and rise to the surface, and concentrates on not glancing over at the shouting man or the arguing barman.

It's not that he doesn't care; he simply doesn't have an opinion. No way of knowing what lies deep in the history of language and culture, and what it might mean to these people. And anyway, it strikes Scott that if you don't like the name of a bar, the easiest thing is not to go in there in the first place.

But different peoples have different cultural baggage, different perspectives on things. They're a funny bunch, these Brits. He has to think for a minute if Brits includes the Irish or not, but he can't remember. All he knows is that there's some confusing business about Great Britain, and the British Isles and the United Kingdom all being different.

Scott sighs and stares at his glass as the argument reaches a new level of energy.

The owner is saying that Paddy just means Patrick, and the Irish guy is asking to see him – to talk to Patrick, the 'supposed' owner.

Scott sips his drink and glances along the bar. He thought a straight pub might be more interesting; he thought it might be a better place to talk to real Brits, to find out what they're thinking, what makes them tick. For that is Scott's thing – people, and what they think.

Some travel to see things, to capture and take home in photographic form the Taj Mahals and the Niagara Falls of this world. Others travel to *do* things – to ride the biggest roller coaster, or climb the Eiffel Tower. But though he doesn't know why, though Scott has no idea whether it's genetics, or education, or some weird freak of brain formation, these things have never interested him. His thing is people. His thing is knowing the minutiae of people's day to day lives.

And *voila* the problem with Britain, or England or whatever... Because the Brits just don't give anything away.

In the gay bars people talk just enough to get him home for sex. And that's good. Scott likes sex. But he has learnt that it isn't that different wherever you go. Sure, it's different from partner to partner, from tribe to tribe, but not truly from country to country. Gay culture is pretty homogenous these days and whether it be New York, Chicago, or London there will be the same tribes. The same dingy leather bars, the same executives in wine bars, the same giggling retail queens huddled in the nearest bar to the gym. Sure, Americans are all cut, and built. And the Brits, it would seem, virtually never are. But other than that...

He wonders, again, if this whole travelling alone thing isn't a mistake. He wonders again if he shouldn't just change his ticket and go home. But then Britain isn't Europe, he reminds himself. And London probably isn't Britain either.

And in the straight pubs like here, people talk eventually. But it's all Bush and Iraq and global warming. It's all political and Scott wants the personal. Scott longs for a good New York conversation with some stranger in a business suit whose father abused her, and who is having a lesbian affair, and who always keeps a dildo in the refrigerator – just in case. For that's the stuff New Yorkers tell each other.

The Irish guy has left now, and Scott has finished his pint, so he glances at the barman, now standing close by, and points at his glass hopefully.

"Fucking Irish," the barman is saying. "Alcoholics every last one of 'em."

*"Now that,"* Scott thinks, *"is a racist slur."*

The barman raises his chin at Scott's neighbour, apparently expecting a reply.

The guy shrugs. "Hey Matt, I have no opinion," he says in an amused tone.

*"Cute,"* Scott thinks, forcefully reminding himself that he is in a straight bar.

The barman smiles. "Wise man," he says. "You should have been a diplomat. So how's your wife? Haven't seen her for a while."

Scott tunes in – the scent of human life is in the air.

"Not my wife, Matt. Girlfriend. We were *never* married."

The barman nods. "Sorry, I just assumed," he says.

"Anyway, we split," the guy says with a shrug. He looks a little worse for wear. He's drinking whisky.

"Sorry mate, I didn't know," the barman says.

Scott snorts in spite of himself.

They both turn to look at him, the barman slightly aggressively, his neighbour in a vague, drunken, dreamy way.

Suzanne Vega comes on the radio, or jukebox, or whatever the source of the music is – an old song, *Small Blue Thing*. Suzanne Vega is so New York, it makes Scott feel truly homesick. "Sorry guys," he says. "I wasn't listening or anything. I was just thinking about things – stuff in my head," he says, tapping his forehead with his index finger.

"You need a refill there mate?" the barman asks and Scott nods and pushes his change, a banknote with coins piled upon it, back across the bar.

"Can I buy you one?" he asks his neighbour.

But the guy shakes his head. "Nah. I've had enough I think," he says. "Thanks all the same."

"So what happened Sime?" the barman asks, as he waits for the tap to fill Scott's glass.

"Nothing," the guy says. "She left. That's all."

Scott snorts again, and both men turn to look at him.

"Hey I'm sorry guys, I'm just…" he sighs. "Look; I was just thinking about how, you know, *private* you Brits are."

The barman raises an eyebrow and hands him his drink. He lifts four coins from the pile, slides the remainder back to Scott, and moves off towards the till.

"Private?" the guy next to him says.

Scott nods. "Yeah, I mean, you two know each other right?"

"I drink here, that's all," he replies.

"Yeah, but you're on first name terms." Scott shakes his head. "I'm sounding weird here. I'm just interested, you know, in all the cultural differences – between here and home. And where I come from, no one would ever just say, you know, *she left me.* You'd always get the full horror story. Most people would probably spice it up a bit too. Make it extra-tragic."

Sime nods slowly, maybe thinking about what Scott has said, maybe trying to think of something to say. "So where's home?" he asks eventually.

"New York," Scott says. "I'm not saying it's, you know, better or worse or anything. But it's real different."

The guy nods again and frowns slightly.

"I kind of collect thoughts," Scott tells him. He half lifts a little pocket book from his breast pocket and then lets it drop back out of sight. "Only no one here seems to tell me anything," he says, grinning dumbly and hunching his shoulders. "So not much to write."

His neighbour tips his head to one side and squints. "So what kind of stuff do people tell you?" he asks.

Scott pulls his pocket book out and flicks through it. "All sorts really ... general stuff, personal stuff. Sometimes it's quite... Here," he says. "MindBar, NY, twelve February. Woman in thigh high PVC boots. "It all started with my uncle. Truth was I enjoyed it. And really, it wasn't the act as such; it was the guilt that wrecked my life, the guilt that I, you know, enjoyed it so much. That and the fact that I've been trying to match it, the sex we had, ever since."

Scott stares at the page a moment, and then flips the book shut. "That's just..." he shrugs. "So ugly and, the honesty is so ... *beautiful*, you know?"

The guy nods. "Wow," he says. "I *do* know, Scott. I know exactly what you mean." He holds out his hand. "Simon," he says.

Scott takes his hand. "Scott."

"So what, you're a writer?" Simon asks him. "You publish this stuff?"

Scott shakes his head. "Nah," he says. "I'm in IT. This is just a hobby. A weird hobby I guess."

Simon nods. "There are worse things to do," he says. "Like abusing your nieces."

Scott nods and smiles weakly. "I guess."

"So what do you want to know?"

Scott wrinkles his brow. "Oh, no. Really. I wasn't ... I mean ... I was just noticing that no one tells me anything, and then, kind of noticing that you guys don't seem to say much to each other either."

Simon nods and sips at his whisky. "OK, but, what would you *like* me to tell you?"

Scott shrugs. "I just like to know people better I guess, I..."

"OK, ask me a question. Anything. I'm tipsy. Make the most of it."

Scott grins and blushes slightly. "OK," he says. "Why did she leave you? Your girl."

Simon smiles a broad, tight-lipped smile, and blinks very slowly. "Money ... mainly," he says eventually. "She came into quite a lot. She became ... quite rich, I suppose.

That's the problem really. And it changed her. So we became different. Because of money."

"You couldn't keep up with her?" Scott says, nodding slowly.

Simon shrugs. "In a way. But it was more, that, we … became different, because of money. She wanted big and shiny. And I…" He shrugs again. "I didn't … don't … care."

Scott nods.

"And you're right by the way."

"I'm sorry?"

"We don't – talk, that is. I mean, no one asked me. None of my friends asked me why we split. You're the first."

Scott scratches his head. "Wow," he says. "So are you sad? Or did it feel right?"

Simon shrugs and smiles coyly. "I guess it was time. To make a break, that is. I miss her, I mean, it becomes a habit, and I *do* love her. Or I love who she *used* to be. But," he blows through his lips. "No regrets, not really."

"And sex? Do you miss that? I mean, that's a habit too. We gay guys, you know, it's pretty easy. I mean, you go to a bar, you pick up some guy…"

Simon smirks. "Yeah, I know," he says. "I have – how do they say it? I have swung both ways, in the past. So I know."

Scott raises an eyebrow. "Wow, a *real* bisexual?"

Simon looks around the bar.

"Sorry," Scott apologizes. "I have a tendency to be too loud."

"You all do," Simon says, blinking deliberately and nodding his head. "All Americans have that tendency. But it's fine."

"Where did she get her money from? I mean, was it family, someone's estate? gambling?"

Simon shakes his head. "She earned it. She's in TV."

"And you?"

Simon laughs dryly. "I am a writer – for TV as well, but a writer, so..."

Scott nods. "Ha!" he says. "You guys are *always* broke."

Simon laughs. "Are we? *I* am. But I'm not sure we *all* are."

"My best friend – back in the States – he's a writer. He's always broke too."

Simon nods and sighs.

"So, let me get you another," Scott says, pointing at Simon's glass.

Simon shakes his head. "No," he says. "I need to go." He pushes his barstool back and stands. He has to blink repeatedly to make his eyes focus properly.

"Well, it was nice talking to you," Scott says, feeling a pang of disappointment at Simon's departure.

Simon pats his shoulder. "You too; have a good trip."

Scott smiles and nods. "You get home safely."

"Oh, I live just..." Simon points vaguely through one of the walls of the bar, then changes his mind and points the other way. "Well, not far anyway," he says, his hand dropping to his side.

Scott watches Simon's back as he walks to the door, and then as the door swings shut, he pulls the book from his pocket to write something down, but hesitates.

He could go after him – try to get an invite for coffee. The idea of a cute bisexual is quite hot really.

The barman looks up from the pint he's serving to see Scott disappearing behind the closing door.

"Yanks," he says. "Worse than the fucking Paddies."

13:55 EASTERN STANDARD TIME

# A New Religion

Tube train – London. On my way home from Simon's place – tiny bed-sit, but great sex. Overheard following conversation between pink-haired fifty-something American punk lady and black-booted Scottish goth. How cool are these two?

Pink – "I know, but it's so bizarre, you know? That someone as normal as him should believe all that Scientology crap."

(Girl is holding a trashy magazine with a photo of John Travolta).

Guy – "I don't know. Is it bizarre? Scientology I mean? I'm not sure you should, you know, *diss* someone else's religion."

"Oh come on. Scientology is awesomely bizarre. It was all invented by this science fiction writer, Ron Hubbard? They believe that we're all spirits from outer space, called *Thetans*. And we, like, came here on a space ship and were put into volcanos. And when the volcanoes erupted the spirits flew out and inhabited the humans."

"Really?"

"Really!"

"OK, so that's bizarre. How come you know so much?"

"Oh I went through this religious phase. I decided I needed some spirituality in my life. And I trawled through all the religions. I got into Scientology because I thought Travolta was hot."

"*Travolta?*"

"It was a long time ago. And then I tried … Buddhism. Yeah, Buddhism was next. But all that Karma shit. Did my head in. I went to Thailand and studied with these monks. But they're always saying, you know, that other people's suffering is all their own fault. I remember pointing at this child prostitute in Chang Mai and asking why someone doesn't do something about it. And this head monk guy told me that she must be paying a Karmic debt, from a previous life. And I thought, no. Not for me. In the end that's just another bullshit religion designed to keep the masses passive."

"Thailand, wow!"

"The monks were hot though. They were wearing orange robes. Like the Krishnas."

"Did you try that one too?"

"Sure. And more. The Raelians. They were too funny. They believe that God is an extra-terrestrial. They need everyone to give them money so they can build like a big airport, or more of a spaceport I guess, so that he can land. That's why he hasn't been back. He's waiting for the spaceport to be built."

"Wow. And do people do it? Do people give them money?"

"Sure, they have, like, millions of adepts. But they are into free love. Which is cool."

"So did you choose one?"

"No. They're all OK on the surface, but there's always some dumb-ass belief that, really, no one believes. But my brain doesn't work that way. It says, either it's True or it isn't. You know?"

"What about the ordinary ones. I mean, why not a sensible religion, like C of E or something?"

"Water into wine? Loaves and fishes? The animals went in two by two? Oh *please.*"

"Yeah, I guess."

"No I made up my own religion in the end. The Church of Cindy. It has two rules. *Strive to Survive Causing the Least Harm…*"

"That's Crass."

"Yeah, I was *so* into Crass."

"I used to have *Penis Envy* – on cassette. Only it disintegrated."

"Cassettes were so lame. I still have it on vinyl. But *Christ – The Album* is better."

"So what are the other rules, in the Church of Cindy?"

"There are only two rules. Strive to survive causing the least harm. And sex – lots of sex. As much sex as possible."

"I am so into you Cindy."

"I know, hey, this is our stop isn't it?"


The truly weird thing, is that I saw the same guy (and I'm sure it *was* the same guy), a couple hours later. He was sitting on a park bench and his mascara had run all down his cheeks – he was weeping. I nearly spoke to him, but he gave me this *fuck you* look, so I chickened out. I wonder what happened?

13:55 EASTERN STANDARD TIME

# So Repressed

Joe turns his head to one side. It's easier to breathe this way.

He's suddenly not so sure about this chick. He's suddenly not sure that he trusts her enough. Sweat prickles on his forehead.

Sure he knew she was going to be weird. But Joe likes weird chicks. Weird chicks are Joe's speciality. He strains against the restraints but he knows there's no way he can get out of them – all that happens is the rope cuts into the skin a little more.

A wave of terror swells deep within, making him feel hot and feverish.

In an effort to distract himself from what is going on behind, namely a wet finger sliding up and down his rim, he lists his previous weird girlfriends. Julia, convinced that nuclear war was imminent – *spend each day as if it's your last, because it probably is...* Kate, the skinny fruitarian – he alternated between being accused of murder and sneaking down the street for his veggie burgers; Janet with whom he watched so many Discovery Channel programmes about aliens that he began to agree that they probably *did* exist...

"Ouch."

The biker chick, whatever her name was, with her leather gear and the huge Harley Davidson look-alike (only it was really a gutless 125…)

"Relax," Cindy tells him. "Don't be so repressed. Give yourself over to pleasure."

He wonders if it's his fault that he can't see the pleasure in having Cindy, who is admittedly hot, that he can't see the pleasure in having Cindy's finger up his arse. It mainly just makes him want to shit. Or fart.

Joe strains at the restraints in a good-natured kind of way. "Jesus, Cindy," he says. "Go easy down there."

He flashes back to his childhood bedroom, and glances across at the wall to check that the Barry Sheen poster isn't there. "*Weird,*" he thinks.

As Cindy withdraws, spits, and forces two fingers in, he groans in a less good-natured way. She's gonna have to realise at some point that there are limits as to what will fit up his backside, and the sooner the better.

"Don't tell me no one's ever been up here before," Cindy laughs. "Don't tell me you're a virgin!"

But no one *has* ever been up there before, well, other than an occasional suppository, and then only ever his mother. Never his step-dad, never a doctor, and never a chick. And he never considered that this made him a virgin. It simply never crossed his mind that anyone could consider it in that way.

"Shit Cindy!" he says.

She gave him a choice – back or front – and he chose badly. He wishes he had chosen *front*. What could she have done then, other than suck him to death? And how bad could *that* be?

"Can I turn over now?" he asks again, straining to look back at her.

Cindy pulls her fingers out and slaps his arse, hard. It feels good. He gets hard again. That's a surprise, that he likes it. He feels himself blush at the realisation.

"Not yet," she says. "I haven't finished with you, not by a long stretch!" Her voice is menacing yet sexy. Sure this is all weird, but at least it's not boring. There's nothing worse than boring.

Cindy slides slowly up his back, licking the length of his spine as she does so. He can feel her breasts following in the wake of her tongue, dragging along and up the length of his back, until they are pressing against his neck and her tongue is in his ear. She slides a hand beneath him and grasps his dick. "Hmmm, me thinks ye protest too much," she says. "Doesn't seem to me like you're hating this *at all*."

She slides sideways so that her face is beside him on the pillow and kisses him deeply. "Are you?" she asks.

His fear recedes and – despite himself – he breaks into a grin.

"Gotcha," Cindy laughs, turning and lowering her head beyond the edge of the bed.

He looks at the back of her head, at the shiny nylon aspect of her pink hair, and wonders for the first time if it's a wig.

"No," she says, as if answering the thought. She fumbles in a drawer below the bed. "I haven't finished at all." When she resurfaces she's holding a gag, two rubber straps with what looks like a golf ball in the middle. "This'll shut you up," she laughs, moving backwards and sitting on his buttocks.

Absurdly he thinks of the ping-pong table in the family home. He remembers hunting for lost balls in the shrubbery. He remembers pretending not to find the balls, pretending to search and search, anything rather than go back inside.

"Cindy, I don't think I want…" But it's too late. She has pulled it between his teeth. His mouth is stuffed with a ping-pong ball for fucks sake. There is nothing left to say.

As she fastens the buckles behind his head, she says, "You guys, so repressed, it's so hard for you to just submit and take the pleasure. So hard for you to let a woman take the lead."

Joe's mouth is salivating around the ball. He can feel saliva dribbling from the corner of his mouth. He frowns at Cindy's logic. It seems to Joe that he *is* submitting. It's the pleasure aspect he's waiting for.

"Well today sweetie, you get to discover a secret," Cindy says, laying her weight across his back again as she fiddles again in the drawer. "You get to find out something that maybe only thirty percent of men ever find out. You get to find out just how good it feels … to…"

As she grapples with the contents of the drawer, her body – specifically her chest – kneads his back. Unable to find what she's looking for, she slips to the floor and kneels beside the bed so that she can pull the drawer fully open.

Joe's eyes widen.

Cindy is pointing a big – *really* big, thick – *really* thick, pink, plastic penis at him.

Joe shouts, *"No!"* Well, to the best of his ability he shouts. He writhes too. He isn't *thinking* or *wondering* about this anymore. This isn't mental-Joe inside his brain calculating, *"Do I fancy this or not?"* or *"Am I up for this new experience?"* No this is the brute, instinctive, *animal* Joe saying – or at least trying his very hardest to say, or if not say, express through his body language – that *this isn't going to happen.*

"Yes," Cindy says, unruffled. "You get to find out ... just how it feels ... to be fucked senseless."

Joe gulps and groans and gags. There can be no mistaking his meaning, but Cindy carries on impervious. She sounds like she thinks this is all part of the game.

Joe starts to sweat freely as Cindy squirts something cold and slippery against his arse and runs the smooth end of her plastic penis up and down the valley between his butt-cheeks.

His fever reaches a new level. He drifts almost unconscious. He's in his childhood bedroom – is he ill? Does he have a fever? Is he waiting for the doctor?

He returns to the here and now and writhes again and shouts through his nose.

"Shhh," Cindy laughs. "You'll have my room-mate in here – or is that what you want? You *dirty* boy."

Joe's eyesight is clouding around the edges now, tinting pink in the centre. He wants to kill Cindy. He wants to break free and beat the bitch to a pulp. He wants to equalize every evil deed that the strong have ever done to the weak. He wants to wipe her stupid grinning pink-haired feminist face from this earth.

Cindy starts to push in the end of the dildo, twisting and turning it as it enters him. "Hmm, this is opening up nicely," she says saucily. "Are you *sure* you never…"

And then Joe is gone from there. He's drifting above his body, watching from on high. And Cindy doesn't look like Cindy. Cindy looks like…

For a split second some other part of him, some part that is watching him lying there in his bedroom, lying there in front of the Barry Sheen poster, the spectator Joe, thinks he may actually be dying, may actually be seeing his life pass before his eyes; maybe he's having a heart attack, or maybe it's just an acid flashback. If he's lucky.

And now he is back and he's standing. The headboard – ripped from the bed yet still strapped between his wrists – is suspended behind his head. What was once the foot of the bed is now snapped into two almost equal sized lumps, each tethered ball-and-chain-like to an ankle.

The clouding of his vision is fading; his hearing – like a momentarily failed soundtrack – slowly returns, and he is shocked at what he sees, shocked at what he hears. Surprise doesn't begin to cover it.

He's stunned to see that he is not in his childhood bedroom but back in this woman's flat. Shocked to see the woman – looking scared – cowering naked in the corner of the room. Shocked to see the entire contents of her bookcase stagger and slide to the floor as one end of his flailing headboard bashes into it and it totters and falls, crashing into and taking the halogen lamp with it.

By the time Joe's rage has subsided, by the time his inexplicable fury has turned to icy hatred – hatred of himself born of embarrassment, and hatred of her for making this happen – the room is truly trashed.

Cindy is still in the corner, her knees drawn before her, trembling. Joe's limbs are still strapped to the splintered remains of the bed.

They sit, silently staring each other out for what seems like hours, but is in fact only a few minutes and then, eventually, Cindy moves, standing and advancing towards him, stepping through the rubble, her palms raised, like a nervous policeman approaching a hostage taker, or maybe someone walking in zero gravity.

She releases his hands and feet first, and then she removes the gag. She winces as she does so, as if anticipating a deluge of insults, a fresh wave of anger or madness, but Joe remains silent.

As he dresses, pulling on his black jeans and tremblingly lacing his thirty-six hole boots, Cindy sits on the lopsided mattress and watches him warily. He can feel the gel she applied sticking clammily to his boxer shorts. And then, he opens the door to her apartment, takes one last glance back, and steps outside.

Everything beyond the threshold of Cindy's door – the orange carpet of the hallway, the grey, ribbed metal of the elevator – it all looks strange. It all seems to have too much detail, like looking through glasses that are a fraction too strong.

He feels like there's a plate of glass between him and his surroundings, he feels like he's in a dream, he feels the way he felt when his stepfather died.

And in a way he just did die. All over again.

Only this time Joe remembers. He remembers everything that happened in front of the Barry Sheen poster. And it hurts. It hurts more than anything ever hurt.

He will never see Cindy again. He will never have to explain to her. Thank God! The bitch would revel in being the one to have liberated his repressed memories.

And maybe he can forget again. For wasn't it better, not remembering? Wasn't it nature's way of protecting him?

He steps out onto the busy London street and tries to remember which way the tube station was.

# Not Quite Unhappy

The screen flashes momentarily and then settles into the whiter than white of a kitchen ad. Jacques looks over the back of the sofa, and shouts, "C'est ton émission chérie," – *It's your programme, dear.*

"Oui, j'arrive," Véronique shouts back.

Jacques settles into the armchair and turns back to face the screen, his complexion pale in the strange light.

"*Off The Grid,*" slides onto the screen.

"Ça commence," Jacques shouts. – *It's beginning.*

"Oui, je suis là," Véronique says, sliding in beside him. "I can't wait to see how they get on."

Jacques slides an arm around her shoulders. "Hey, it's just TV. You got so wrapped up in it last time."

"I know," she says. "But it's based on a true story. The guy who wrote it, well he actually did all of this."

"I kind of doubt that it can be as good as the first series," Jacques says.

Véronique nudges him in the ribs. "Shhh," she says. "Let's watch it, eh?"

"*Off The Grid Supports Plan International. Helping those who never asked to be off the grid,*" the screen says.

"That's new," Jacques comments.

"Yeah," Véronique agrees. "Makes sense though. Quite ironic really. Rich whites choosing to live off the grid. Plan International do those foster children things. I was talking about doing it, do you remember?"

"Yeah," Jacques says as the screen fades and fills with the narrator's head. "Well, you know what I think. I think it's bullshit. Charity bullshit. And charity isn't what they need."

"*Umh,*" Véronique says. "Well, I think it's got to be better than doing nothing."

Jacques shrugs. "Huh!" he says.

"God you're cynical," Véronique says.

"*Jake and Martin fell in love with this log cabin, nestling in the Pocono Mountains, only trouble was, it was off the grid,*" the presenter says.

Jacques scans the subtitles. "I'm glad they didn't dub it again," he says, talking over the programme. "I hate it when they dub it."

Véronique nods. "Yeah," she says. "Now shhhh."

Images of the previous series scroll across the screen, making the subtitles momentarily difficult to read. "... but now, winter is upon them," says the narrator. "And it is a winter the like of which Jake and Martin have never seen before."

As the screen turns white, his face disappears into the glare. Slowly the log cabin appears, barely perceptible beneath a snowdrift. "Mon Dieu!" Véronique says, as the image cuts to Jake peering through the kitchen window at the whiteness of the snow. *"Hey Martin,"* he says. *"It, erm, snowed a bit in the night. You need to like, come and look at this."*

After the programme ends, after Jacques has gone to bed, Véronique sits quietly and wonders. She wonders if Jake and Martin – or whatever the real couple are called – were / are really that happy. She wonders, again, whether such real solidity, such contentment, exists in other people's relationships. In short, she wonders if couples like Jake and Martin have to go through the same shit that she does.

It's not that Véronique is unhappy. For Véronique has known unhappiness, like the bored emptiness before she met Jacques, the long winter evenings when she felt she was on the verge of bashing her brains out against the kitchen window, just to stop being bored. So yes, she's known unhappiness, and so she knows she's not unhappy. But she's not quite happy either. Because she has also known the state of pure happiness too, and this isn't that either. This is nearly happy. Or, if you prefer, not quite *unhappy*. And she wonders if that is good enough. She wonders if accepting the permanent, comfortable, average state that is this relationship... Well, she wonders if it isn't like selling your soul to the devil, as if accepting mediocre sex, and accepting a pleasant dull life, in a pleasant dull apartment, with a pleasant dull man... No, that's not fair. But Véronique wonders if accepting this compromise relationship is actually saving her from the blinding unhappiness of being alone, or if it merely precludes the reorganisation of her life and the meeting of a true soul mate that she really needs.

Of course, sometimes, Véronique really *is* happy with Jacques, even *because* of Jacques. What makes her happiest is when she, very occasionally, manages to make Jacques happy. And she hates herself for this. It seems such a stupid, feminine, *submissive* thing to do. To make one's happiness dependant on that of her husband. But it does. Making Jacques happy makes Véronique happy.

And therein lies the crux of the problem. For does that not mean that Véronique *loves* Jacques? This is the proof, isn't it? Isn't that the very nature of love? That what makes Véronique most happy in the whole world, is being able to make Jacques happy?

But she doesn't seem to manage it very often. *"Jacques est abonné au malheur,"* she thinks. – *Jacques has a subscription to unhappiness.* His life, it seems to her, is set up as a series of dichotomous pairings of desire and action. So whatever Jacques truly wants is the one thing Jacques can't or won't obtain. Jacques wants to be thin, but he can't stop eating. And he wants to be fit, but he won't stop smoking. And he wants better sex. But he can't talk about it. And he hates the city, but his job ties him to Paris … and on and on and on.

Véronique is more pragmatic, maybe even a little simple. She does things she likes, and doesn't do things she hates. And when she wants something she can't get – for *sure*, she would *love* to look like Kate Winslett – she sighs, regrets, and lets it go.

If you're busy enough getting what you do want, she figures; if you're working towards the things that *are* within grasp, then there just isn't time for worrying about the unobtainable.

So Jacques' life, it feels to Véronique, is taut like a rubber band about to snap. And she tries to find solutions, tries to come up with ways they could move out of the city, suggests career options so that Jacques can leave his job, suggests new sexual positions they could try. But Jacques always comes up with a reason why. "Oui, mais…" he will say. "Yes but." And though Véronique can fight off any number of objections standing in the way of happiness, in the end she always ends up giving in. Jacques' resistance to change always beats her, always leaves her feeling that her own view of life is over simplified, a little autistic even. It's as if the idea that you can like what you do, and not do what you don't like, is somehow vacuous or dumb. Life just isn't that simple, Jacques seems to be saying.

And sometimes, like now, she begins to wonder if Jacques isn't *already* doing what he likes best. She wonders if being unhappy with his lot isn't maybe the thing that Jacques enjoys the most. Maybe that's why he does it all the time.

No that's harsh. Jacques isn't unhappy *all* the time. But he's never quite happy either.

And Véronique in all of that? Frankly she doesn't care about much – the details of where they live and how they earn a living, of what they wear and who they see, honestly don't matter to her that much. All she really wants is to spend her time with someone she can make happy. Someone who wants to be happy. And sometimes, like now, she wonders if she hasn't simply chosen the wrong guy.

# 13:55 EASTERN STANDARD TIME

# Virtual Reality

Jacques closes his eyes and concentrates, his hand resting on his dick. Partly out of guilt, and partly as a mental exercise, he tries to conjure up images of Véronique, but he sees her driving or in the kitchen, and that doesn't really do it for him.

She's only next door – he can hear her moving around – so he could just go and get her, could even just call out her name and she would come running, flattered and eager.

He tries, in his mind's eye, to dirty her up a bit, to give her shiny lip-gloss and high heels, but she morphs into someone else entirely, a random image of the dirty-girl he never slept with. And that's the problem, because, in truth, Jacques would rather have virtual reality sex with this figment of his imagination, than actual sex with his wife.

It's not that there's anything wrong with Véronique. She's pretty, kind, clever. She's an attractive enough woman. But Jacques' sexuality revolves more around physical specifics than personality. High boots, for example. The girl in his mind's eye totters into the bedroom wearing thigh high leather boots. A cliché Jacques knows, but what can he say? It does it. And glossy red lipstick. And big pert breasts. The girl is morphing into Véronique's trashy friend Olivia. As usual.

He doesn't know why these things turn him on this way, and wonders briefly, if somewhere in the world, some psychologist has explained why people get turned on by specifics – in his case, boots, silky blouses, breasts, lipstick...

So, no, he doesn't know why these things make him hard – his dick is twitching and quivering now – but they do. Véronique knows about it all of course. And she disapproves. She thinks it's all cheap and tacky. So does he, to tell the truth. And she thinks it's to do with him being a sexist pig – wanting to turn her into a sex object, she says. She thinks he should be able to decide that what turns him on is Véronique in a dressing gown stroking his forehead and telling him she loves him. Véronique also wants more sex, better sex; but she wants it on her own terms. Shame. Because it doesn't matter – sex-wise – how sweet Véronique is, or how much fun they have on holiday, or how much she loves him, because none of that makes his dick hard. Whereas Olivia, well!

So where's the harm? Where's the harm in living with Véronique and having virtual reality sex with Olivia in his head? Véronique would be mortified if she knew, but of course she never will. Unless he says her name in his sleep – he worries about that sometimes. But otherwise, well, what Véronique doesn't know can't hurt her, can it? And it's not like he's actually doing anything wrong, is it?

In a way, it *is* problematic, he realises. Because this is actually the first thing he ever decided to *not* tell Véronique about, and in some weird moral way, it feels like it probably *is* as bad as actually cheating on her. But as long as she doesn't find out then the moral imperative of not hurting those one loves remains intact.

His hard-on is fading, so he spits on his hand and rubs a little harder, and wonders if the moral imperative thing applies to actual affairs too; if he had an *actual* affair with slutty Olivia, and Véronique didn't know, could anyone really claim that he had hurt her?

Now *there's* a fantasy!

# 13:55 EASTERN STANDARD TIME

## More Myself Or Less Myself

Véronique sits on the red Ikea sofa, the box of photos between her legs. She swallows hard and pulls another cliché from the box. This time it shows Jacques sitting on a donkey, grinning madly. His legs look pale and spindly, his eyes – terrified.

She pulls another from the box. Jacques in a sombre blue suit standing next to their artist friend, Federico at a private view. Dressed up, Jacques looks tall and proud, noble even. He holds himself differently when he wears a suit; she likes it. She has tried to get him to dress up more often, but he says it's not him, says it makes him feel like a bank manager.

She runs a finger across the photo and something stirs within – whether it's love or desire she's not quite sure.

She wipes a hand across her mouth, and blinks to dispel a forming tear. So much time together, so many memories. And the truth is that it really isn't *all* bad – far from it. And after five years together – fifteen percent of her entire life thus far – five years of holidays and shopping trips, birthdays and arguments... After all that, Jacques feels like a *part of her.*

The idea of leaving him, though, feels liberating all the same, feels like a last chance for a different life, a better life.

Opportunity served up on a plate. A final chance to be who she really is, to return to the source of who, or what, Véronique Delanoe is, was, can be. Young and proud and independent again. Sad and lonely and scared again.

She thinks of a song lyric, an English lyric from her favourite band, *Everything But The Girl*. – *How am I without you? Am I more myself or less myself? I feel younger, louder, like I don't always connect.*

She realises that she is staring at the wall, and pulls her focal point back to the box of photos and delves anew.

She and Jacques in Venice, laughing – rather stupidly it seems now – at the unknown delay of the self-timer on the camera. They had a big row right afterwards; but even that, even the arguments, even Jacques' own failings feel like they belong, feel almost as much a part of her as her own shortcomings, and God knows, she has plenty.

But some things can't be forgiven can they? Not without loss of face by the forgiving party. One can't, surely, accept anything, everything, can one? And if she does? If she does just say, "Whatever you have done, I forgive you, I want you so much, I love you so much, that I accept your failure. I would rather live with the disappointment of who you are than find myself alone again." Well what does that make her? *Forgiving?* Broad-minded? Or just desperate, needy, co-dependant?

She slides the picture back in and flips quickly through a wad of dull photos – a holiday house, a dog, a car... And then, there it is – the perfect allegory for their relationship.

She is on the right, looking confused or puzzled by something happening off-frame. Jacques is standing, hands in pockets on the left, smiling the cheap plastic smile of holiday shots. And beside him, too blurred to make out, someone else, blurred because she's moving into, or out of the picture – the unknown woman. Véronique wonders. Is she moving *into*, or *out of* the picture?

# 13:55 EASTERN STANDARD TIME

# Choose Your Own Truth

Olivia raises an eyebrow expectantly and takes a deep, almost aggressive drag of her cigarette. The tobacco crackles. "So are you going to leave him?" she asks.

"I don't know," Véronique says quietly, staring across the restaurant at the guy rolling out the pizza bases.

"But you said you weren't happy before. And now, with this, well I just assumed..." Olivia says, her voice plaintive, disappointed even.

Véronique frowns at her friend and wonders why single friends always egg you towards separation, whilst couples always encourage you to stay together. Is it because they just assume that they themselves have made the better choice? That they are the model to follow? Or is it because they are jealous, because they hate to see you have what they do not, whether that be freedom, fun, stability or love?

"I know," Véronique says.

"Jesus, if any guy cheated on me," Olivia says shaking her head.

"I know," Véronique says again, thinking, *"That's why you're single."*

"I mean, if I think about it... If I think about the mechanics of him actually being with someone else, whoever she is, you know, the physicality of his body with someone else's... Well, it's a no-brainer really. I *have* to leave him."

Olivia nods. "Exactly," she says.

"But then I think about how sad he was when he told me, how easy it is to get drunk and do something you regret, and he's so sad now, and I do *hate* to see him sad ... and then I think, say, how good my birthday was..."

"When he took you to Italy?"

Véronique nods. "Or, if I think about how we laugh at the same things, how we like the same tunes... If I think about all *that* stuff, then I feel that I couldn't *possibly* leave him."

Olivia sighs – apparently bored by this complexity – and glances over her shoulder towards the kitchen. "I'm starving," she says, then, turning back to face Véronique, "So?"

Véronique shrugs again. "I don't know. I thought those two thoughts would somehow merge. That one would win out over the other. That they would melt into each other and the result would be me knowing what to do. But they don't. They haven't."

"And in the meantime, you're still there."

Véronique nods. "The advantage of incumbency," she says.

Olivia glances at the kitchen again and then pulls another Chesterfield from the packet. "Incumbency?" she repeats.

"Yeah ... I mean, there are three possibilities. You choose to stay, or you choose to leave, or you don't choose at all. It's a two out of three chance that you stay. Because if you don't choose then you end up staying as well, don't you."

"That's what mistresses never learn," Olivia says. "The husbands *never* leave the wives."

"Exactly," Véronique says. "Well, two out of three don't. But I don't want to *not* choose; I want to decide. To forgive and stay and be happy. Or to leave."

"And be happy," Olivia adds.

Véronique nods. "Well, yes."

"And? What does your heart tell you?"

Véronique shrugs. "I don't know. It just goes round and round. If I think about the cheating and the lies, and the boring nights in front of the TV, then my heart tells me to go."

"Ah, so in your heart of hearts you think…"

"But," Véronique interrupts. "If I think about my birthday, or last Christmas, or the fact that we laugh at the same things, and want to go and see the same films, and… So if I think about all the good stuff, or the stuff that's OK at any rate, then my heart tells me to stay."

Olivia shakes her head. "You think about things too much Véro, really you do."

Véronique shrugs. "I have to. Because in the end *I* have to choose."

"I think it's your heart that should decide."

"Yeah, and it will. But I have to choose which bit to think about. And I know that if I think about the bad stuff, then that's one reality. And it's the end, then, isn't it. And if I think about the good stuff, and it's just as true, then it will last, we'll get through this. And there are two lives at stake here." She glances up at the waiter and smiles and nods and reaches out for her pizza. "That's mine," she says. "Merci."

She wonders suddenly if that's what philosophers mean when they say that reality is an illusion; that everyone chooses their own reality. She thinks about mentioning this to Olivia, but decides she wouldn't get her point.

Once the waiter has deposited the pizzas and headed off she continues, "There are two lives here, and we're at a fork in the road, and I have to turn the wheel. Even though it's Jacques' fault that we're here, I still have to choose what to think, what to believe, which way to go. And that's a responsibility. That's hard, Olivia. That's really hard."

As Véronique walks home, she thinks again about the fickle nature of truth. She pauses in front of a department store and alternates between looking at her own reflection, watching the window-dresser - cute and patently gay - as he empties the display, and following the reflections of cars sweeping past behind her.

She wonders again why Olivia is being so negative, why she is encouraging her so to leave? It makes her feel uncomfortable to think about it, as if she has detected something unsavoury in her friend's psyche. And then it dawns on her. Just as she herself can choose between thinking about the positive or negative aspects of her relationship, and just as her own gut feelings change as she does so, so Olivia must be focusing on the negative, and her reaction, her advice is simply the result of her own, honest, gut reaction. And maybe she's not even choosing. Maybe some people - the people who stay in the same relationship from adolescence to death – have brains that naturally dwell on the positive, that naturally think about all the reasons to stay. And then others, like Olivia, have a mindset that constantly seeks out the negative. That would certainly explain why their advice is always, *get out*, always *run!* Véronique nods at the thought and turns towards home. It would explain too, why Olivia is *always* single. Well, single or unsatisfactorily, tragically dating. Or splitting up.

Véronique pulls a chair up at the kitchen table and pulls a sheet of paper and a pen from the drawer behind her. She flattens the blank page with her hand and then writes, "Noel," at the top. – *Christmas.*

Only two weeks to go and she hasn't even thought about what to do, where to go, who to buy for... As if her indecision about Jacques has spread to every area of her life. She writes, "Gifts."

But *who* to buy for? Mum, – *sure.* Olivia – *no doubt.* But what about Jacques? And there the thought processes grind to a halt. And isn't this what happens with *every* aspect of Christmas?

Because how can you plan anything for the future until you decide who you are spending that future with? How can she shop for Christmas food or gifts, until she knows if she is spending it here, with Jacques, or back home with her parents?

She lays the pen down, and clasps her hands around her nose. *Jacques.* Is this a temporary halt in a life-long journey or the end of the line?

She reaches for the pen again and doodles tiny squares around the edge of the page. The past weeks have been so exhausting. Jacques has exhausted his capacity for apology, and Véronique can no longer listen to it anyway. And it always ends up with Jacques, looking at her expectantly, like a puppy waiting for the bone to be handed over. It always ends with Jacques saying, "So, are we OK, now?" And that makes her angry. Of course they're not OK. If she could make it all suddenly OK she would. Only she doesn't know how. And yet – as two months of this bullshit testify – she doesn't know how to leave yet either.

She runs her pen around the edge of the "Noel," heading again, and then scribbles it out and writes, "Jacques," instead. She divides the page into two columns and puts plus and minus symbols at the top.

"Funny," she writes, in the plus column. She glances behind as if nervous that someone will catch her, even though Jacques is at work and she knows she has the flat to herself.

"Gets on with family and friends, great birthday gifts, organises great surprises, likes good music, laughs at the same jokes, looks cute – esp. in a suit, body still OK, great dick, nice bum, generous, says he loves me, says he's sorry, great cook, good at fixing things…"

She smiles, nods slowly and raises the end of the pen to her lips. It's not such a bad list. She's known worse. She has known much worse. She feels a wave of warmth for him, feels convinced that were he here, at this instant, she could do nothing but hug him and say, *"Yes, OK, let's carry on."*

She exhales through her nose, sets her jaw, and moves her pen to the *minus* column.

"Unfaithful," she writes. "Always dissatisfied."

She taps her finger nervously against the shank of the pen and runs her tongue across her teeth. All her feelings of happiness have vanished, like the warm air sucked out of an open window.

It's just too complicated to think about. The two columns are too diametrically opposed to inhabit the same page. The feelings those thoughts generate are too disparate to inhabit the same *mind*. And the opposition of these two halves of the truth is driving her insane. Truly *insane*, she now realises.

She stares at the table until her eyes drift out of focus, then fingers the letters she has set aside for Jacques. They are all printed, official letters – bank statements or bills. Except one handwritten envelope. She strokes her finger across it thoughtfully, feeling guilty already about what she is about to do. And then she rubs her fingers together, glances behind once again, and lifts it to the light.

She instantly sees that the letter within is printed; sees a big blue logo at the top of the page. And then she recognises the logo – sees that it is Plan International, the charity. She smiles. So that's what Jacques is giving her for Christmas.

She slides the envelope back into the pile and returns her gaze to the list, making, in that split second, the decision that has eluded her until now.

With a rapid-fire battery of vertical and horizontal strokes, she scribbles over the two entries in her minus column until every trace is hidden, and then, still not satisfied, she folds and rips the page down the middle, screwing the minus column into a ball and lobbing it into the dustbin.

Nodding thoughtfully at the bit of truth she has chosen, and almost smiling, she forces herself to reread every word on the page.

*"I choose these thoughts because they make me feel happy,"* she thinks. *"I choose contentment. I choose stability. I choose Jacques."*

She contemplates this for a moment, and then flips the page, determined to banish all bad thoughts from her mind, determined to concentrate on saving Christmas.

So who to buy for? Jacques, Olivia...

Véronique frowns. Jacques and Olivia. She tilts her head to one side, stares into the middle distance and grinds her teeth together. Jacques and Olivia. She wonders why she never thought of it before.

# Part Three

*"Love does not begin and end
the way we seem to think it does.
Love is a battle, love is a war; love is a growing up."*

**– James A. Baldwin**

# 13:55 EASTERN STANDARD TIME

# Frozen

A lice opens her eyes and frowns as she tries to identify the noise which lifted her from her light, cold-tormented sleep. It's not that the noise – a low, mechanical humming – is particularly loud. It's just that the silence of the cabin is so absolute, the rhythmic chugging so out of context.

She reaches out from beneath the heavy quilt and twitches the curtains back. Bright light tinged with blue streams into the bedroom. The sight of her breath rising confirms the data coming from her arm   the room is icy cold. Maybe the noise is some kind of heating; maybe if she just waits a little, it will warm up. But now she's awake she's too hungry to wait and see, so she steals herself against the cold and swings her legs to the floor. The cold, even through her thick, fleecy men's pyjamas, is truly spectacular.

"Jesus!" she mutters. "How can they live like this?"

But as soon as she opens the bedroom door, a wave of warmth washes over her. Feeling a little disgruntled that she has pointlessly spent a sleepless night in a deep freeze – she only had, it seems, to open the door – she pads through to the kitchen.

Will and Jude look up and smile evenly as she enters the room. She wonders briefly if they are laughing at her pyjamas or smiling welcomingly at her, but her sleepy brain is quickly distracted by the smell of coffee.

"We were debating whether to wake you up for breakfast," Jude grins.

"But you're just in time," Will adds.

At the sight of the two men together, at the sound of their shared sentence, a pang of something twinges deep within, and she frowns with a vague sense of irritation, but again, her brain is too slow to take the thought any further and she nods at the coffee pot. "There any coffee in there?" she asks.

Will folds the newspaper – it's the *New York Times* she brought with her yesterday – and reaches behind for a cup. "Sure thing," he says.

Jude, who is standing chopping mushrooms, glances over. "I'm doing a big cooked breakfast," he says.

"Pancakes and all," Will adds.

"How does that sound?" Jude asks.

Alice looks from one to the other, and then, addressing the space halfway between them, she says, "Just fine. That sounds just fine."

"So did you sleep well? We thought you might want to sleep a bit late."

Alice shrugs and takes the mug of coffee Will is offering. She takes a sip – it is bitter and dark, just how she likes it – then says, "I was a bit cold to tell the truth. That bedroom seems to be a bit of an ice-box."

Will swivels to face Jude who wiggles his brow and bites his lip. "Gee, I'm sorry Alice," he says. "I forgot to switch your vent on! You should have said."

"Jesus Alice," Will says. "You must have been frozen. It was eighteen degrees last night."

"I'm so sorry Alice. Why didn't you say something?"

Alice shrugs and shakes her head. "Last time we spoke, you told me the bedrooms were cold. I thought that was how it was supposed to be."

Will shakes his head and laughs. "Poor Alice," he says. "We put central heating in when Jude got his payout. Did you get *any* sleep?"

Alice shrugs again. "A bit, I guess. As long as it will be warmer tonight."

"Will actually stoked the boiler up specially," Jude tells her, now halving tomatoes, and placing them on the grill-pan.

"I knew you'd be cold," Will adds.

She stares out at the thick-snow covering the trees. "Eighteen degrees, you say?"

Will nods, and points at a weather station on the wall. "That's what the machine says," he says.

"And the machine never lies," Jude laughs.

"So how do you heat? I mean, what does it run on?" Alice asks, looking around for the source of the warmth.

"Wood. We have a wood-burning furnace – the latest thing. It's self stoking, so you just load it with wood-pellets twice a day."

"It's completely ecological," Jude says.

"Unlike the generator," Will says, tauntingly.

Alice frowns and listens again. "Is that the low humming sound?" she asks.

Will nods. "The solar panels have iced over again; it's a recurring problem."

"So we have to have the generator on for a day to recharge the batteries," Jude says. "It's very un-ecological, but we've only had it on so far for, what?"

"Three days, four days … so far this winter."

Alice nods and sips her coffee again. "The solar panels ice over you say?" she says.

Will nods. "It only happens when it snows at night."

"And if it's very cold," Jude says.

"If it snows during the day it just melts…"

"Because they're black," Jude says. "They heat up in the sun, so the snow just melts."

"But because it snowed at night, and then just melted a little, and then froze over again…" Will continues.

Jude shakes his head. "So now they're all frozen and white, so even though the sun is out, well, they just *stay* frozen."

"Jude tried to chip it off, but he's scared of breaking them."

"They're made of glass, so…" Jude says, now pouring pancake mix into a bowl.

Alice nods, slightly dazed by the early morning information overload. She stares out of the window again, at the drips forming on the icicles around the black plastic rain-butt outside the window.

"We had new windows put in your bedroom too," Jude says. "Triple glazed ones. It used to be even colder. Imagine!"

"I'd rather not," Alice mutters.

"Yeah, that cash arrived just at the right time," Will laughs. "Just before winter."

Alice swivels back to face them. "Did you get the deal you wanted in the end, Jude?" she asks.

Jude wipes his hands on a cloth and pushes through to the bathroom, mumbling, "A minute, I just..."

Will nods exaggeratedly and replies for him. "He got nearly four hundred thousand dollars," he says.

"Four hundred thousand!" Alice nods, impressed.

"He gave most of it away though," Will tells her. "To charity."

Alice wide-eyes him. "He gave it away?"

"Yeah, it was causing some friction," Will says. "It's hard to explain."

Alice frowns. "What, between you two?"

Will wobbles his head from side to side. "Kind of," he says. "It can be complicated, in a couple, if one of you comes into money... And he was asking me to give up my well paid job so that I could come and live here at the same time, it was creating an imbalance, even though we didn't want it to."

Alice shakes her head. "Wow," she says.

Will nods. "But even with what he kept, well, it cleared all the debt, and we fixed all the stuff that needed fixing."

"Well, yes," Alice says. "Four hundred thousand ... Jude was talking about twenty, I think, when I last spoke to him about it. Good negotiating!"

Will nods. "A stroke of luck," he says. "One of Jude's oldest friends bumped into this guy, in London of all places.

And he knew the production company; he knew what the budget was."

The door to the bathroom creaks and Jude reappears.

"I was just saying what a stroke of luck it was, Scott bumping into that guy in London," Will says.

Jude laughs. "Yeah, amazing! Sure made negotiating easier." He looks at Alice now. "He told us the budget they had set aside, you see."

"Jude was going to settle as low as ten thousand at one point, weren't you doll?"

Jude nods. "Yeah, good old Scott."

Alice nods. "And he just, bumped into... To who exactly?"

"Sucked his cock more like," Will laughs.

"Will!" Jude admonishes. "They *dated*," he explains, turning back to face Alice. "And he, this guy Scott dated in London, Simon is his name, he is like the ex husband of the woman I was negotiating with. Weird huh?"

Alice nods. "Truly bizarre," she says, glancing back out of the window at the rain-butt. "Maybe there is a God."

Jude snorts. "Yeah, well..." he says. "Let's not get into that one."

"No," Will laughs. "Let's not."

"So why can't you just lay something over them – to absorb the sun and melt the snow?" Alice asks.

Will blinks at her. "I'm sorry?"

"Over your solar panels," Alice says. "Why can't you just stretch a black tarp or something over them? And then take it away once the snow has melted, or gone soft, or whatever."

Will frowns at her, then cocks his head to one side and looks at Jude. "Jude?" he prompts.

Jude pulls his gaze away from the skillet and frowns at them both. Then he opens his mouth as if to object, pauses, raises an eyebrow, and finally shrugs and says, "Alice, you're a genius."

Alice shakes her head and pushes out her lips. "Sorry, it just sort of came to me. I was watching the snow melting on your rain-butt."

Will shrugs back. "It's worth a try," he says. "It happens every winter."

"We'll have to go over to Cole's and buy a tarp and some of those elastic things," Jude says. "It could work."

As they drive through the blinding white scenery, Alice sits silently and lets life glide by. It feels pleasant and distant, like a nature programme. Beside her in the cab, Will and Jude twitter and chatter randomly about students at the community college where Will teaches, and ideas for Jude's next novel, and laundry powder, and what to cook for dinner.

Alice doesn't really listen to the words. She's concentrating more on the sound – the gentle bubbling of the conversation between this couple who are so comfortable together, who so clearly love each other, and who through years of living together have got into the irritating habit of finishing each other's sentences.

She's feeling very emotional, she realises, here in the warmth both physical and emotional of the pickup. She's actually feeling almost tearful, a swirl of conflicting emotions fighting for dominance. She's enchanted by the beauty of the surroundings, warmed by the presence of Will and Jude who long ago became her closest friends. But she's also irritated to hell by their cosy chitchat; she feels almost suffocated by it. She watches tree after tree slide past, and decides that it's maybe just lack of sleep, and general end-of-year tiredness, and then she digs a level deeper and vaguely acknowledges that she's jealous. She's forty-two and still doesn't have a partner, still doesn't have someone to sit in the cab of a pickup and talk about laundry soap with. It's like her life has been stuck in a groove, frozen in suspended animation, for the last ten years. Everyone seems to be moving forward, building, planning, going places... Everyone except her.

As they slowly round a bend, pushing through a surprisingly narrow channel between the mounds of snow, Alice sees something dart across the bank. She points, and Will pauses mid sentence to look.

"Fox!" he says.

"He's fast," Alice says. "He's a fast fox."

Maybe detecting something in the tone of her voice, Will raises a hand to stop Jude picking up the previous conversation. "You OK?" he asks her. "You seem kinda quiet."

Alice sighs. "Just thoughtful," she says. "Lack of sleep, and a change of scenery. Makes me think about stuff."

They move onto the highway, and Jude, out of habit, reaches for the dial of the radio. But Will intercepts his hand and pulls it to his lap, causing Jude to glance sideways at him. Alice sees all of this from the corner of her eye and silently sighs.

"So what's wrong Alice?" Will asks her. "Spit it out."

Alice laughs. "Oh, nothing's wrong," she says. "Really."

"OK, so what stuff are you thinking about?"

Alice snorts. "Oh the usual. Why am I still single? That kinda stuff."

Will slides an arm around her shoulders. Alice wonders if it will make her cry.

"Search me," he says. "If I were straight, I'd snap you up, girl."

"I love being here with you guys, but it makes me so darn jealous too," she says quietly. "You're so lucky, you know."

Will squeezes her shoulder, then turns to stare at the highway.

They drive in silence for a few minutes; the only sound the humming of the engine and the sloshing beneath the wheel-arches. "It's not luck though," Jude eventually says. "None of it is luck."

Alice takes this in, nodding slowly to herself. "Sure, I mean, I know you guys work at your relationship," she says. "But you were lucky to meet each other; lucky to meet that significant other. That's all I mean."

After a pause, Jude asks flatly, "You want me to be honest Alice? You want to know why *I* think you're single?"

Alice feels a lump in her throat. Jude's honesty is legendary, and she's not sure she's up to it today. She glances at Will. He's pursing his lips and blowing as if he is making a smoke ring or whistling.

"Jude, I'm not sure that now is quite..." Will says, clearly thinking about the fact that they're all trapped in the cab of this truck, thinking about the fact that he's sandwiched between them.

And then Alice decides, *what the hell.*

"Actually Jude," she says. "If you think you know, then please tell me. There isn't anything I would like to know better."

She sees Will pull a face and squash as far back into the seat as he can.

"It's because you're lazy Alice," Jude says.

"Lazy," Alice repeats flatly.

"Yeah," Jude says. "Lazy."

"I've been called many things, Jude," she says. "But…"

"Only about relationships, mind," Jude continues. "You're not lazy about your job, or lazy about your friends, or lazy about sport. But you *are* lazy about relationships."

Alice pushes her lips out and nods in a non-committal manner. "I think I put quite a lot of effort into it," she says, after a pause. "I've done Internet dating, speed dating, and…"

"Yeah," Jude agrees. "You put plenty effort into meeting people. But none at all into making it work out."

Alice nods again and glances at Will. He is pulling a raised eyebrow, *don't-ask-me* kind of a face.

"But I haven't met anyone significant," Alice protests. "That's all I mean when I say you're lucky. I'm not *getting* at you."

"Sure Alice, Will and I met. We were both in a gay bar and we met. But that's where the luck ends. We met. Just like you met that guy from San Diego."

"Oh, Jude! He was from *San Diego!*" she protests. "He was still with his *wife!*"

"He's not now though, is he," Jude points out.

"But they split *after* he and I split, you know that. I was just... I was just an adventure for him, that's all."

"Is that what he said?"

"He was living *with his wife* Jude. In *San Diego*. It was an affair. It wasn't a significant life-partner kind of thing."

"When Jude and I met, he was living in Chicago, and I was in New York," Will says.

Jude nods. "Yeah, I spent *hours* travelling back and forth, *days*, *weeks*. And then when I wanted to move here, Will had to give up everything to join *me*. That's not luck Alice. That's effort. Do you see what I'm saying here?"

Alice nods. "OK. But it was worth it. Because you love each other."

"And sometimes we hate each other, for days."

"Weeks," Will says.

"Yeah," Alice says. "Well, I've never even seen you have a crossed word."

Will shakes his head. "Alice," he says. "You have *no* idea. We nearly split up when Jude got that money."

"It was terrible," Jude says. "Will went all strange on me."

Will shakes his head. "Yeah, I don't know why that happened really, but it just made me feel..." he shrugs.

Alice nods. "Ok," she says. "So you had what, like, one bumpy patch in how many years?"

"We had others too," Jude says. "Like that one with your brother."

Will rolls his eyes. "Major drama," he says. "My brother drinks a lot, and he had *such* a go at Jude one Christmas."

"They had the biggest row," Jude says. "And I couldn't really say a word."

"And then Jude and I fell out over it too," Will says.

"I didn't think he should be avoiding his brother so... Ooh, it got complicated."

Will shakes his head and sighs. "But not as complicated as you and Luke," he says, a sour note entering his voice.

Jude pulls a face. "No," he says blankly.

Alice frowns. "Luke?"

"Yeah, I cheated on him," Jude says, sheepishly.

Will nods. "That was a major one."

"Will nearly moved out," Jude says.

"Will *did* move out," Will corrects.

Alice shakes her head. "I'm sorry," she says. "I had no idea."

"It was about sex," Jude says. "I was kind of bored and ... Will has this really slutty friend..."

"*Had*," Will corrects. "Luke, a leather queen. But cute. And a complete slut."

"And I got all confused, and thought, you know, as a writer, that I needed to explore the darkest reaches of my sexuality. And then I got it all mixed up and thought I was in love with him," Jude says.

Alice shakes her head. "Is this, you know, since I knew you? Because I really had no idea."

Jude nods. "Yeah… I guess it was kind of private, and for a long time we were just working through it." He shrugs. "And in the end, really it was just sex. That's what I learnt I guess. That sex can be just sex."

"We both had to learn that," Will says, managing to glance fondly at Jude. "But we did, didn't we babe. We got through it."

"Like *you* do when you hate your job," Jude adds. "Because in the end, we just don't think there's a better picture anywhere else. It's as simple as that."

Will squeezes Alice's shoulder again, but she shrugs him away. "So *I'm* single because I don't try hard enough," she says. "That's what you're saying."

Jude sighs sadly. "No, Alice, what I'm saying…"

Alice waits for a moment, and then prompts, "Yeah?"

"I'm just thinking about the words," Jude says. "Hang on…"

Alice stares from the side window and blinks back tears.

"OK, what I'm saying," Jude says. "Is that, I think … maybe… Maybe you think it's *your* job to find someone, and like, God's job to make it significant," Jude says.

Alice swallows and looks back at him. "My job to what? Sorry, I tuned out."

"Never mind," Jude says.

Alice frowns. "No please," she says.

Jude coughs. "OK, maybe you think it's *your* job to find someone and *God*, or life, or the universe or whatever-you-believe-in's job to make it *significant*."

Alice frowns, and then nods. "OK, yeah. Pretty much. And?"

"I'm just saying that it's maybe God's job to find someone, to make someone manifest in your life ... and maybe it's *your* job to make it significant," he says. "I'm just suggesting that it's maybe the other way around."

# The Slowlands

Alice looks around in amazement. "My God!" she exclaims. "I had no idea that places like this still exist."

Jude is grinning at her. "Isn't it great!" he says, taking her by the elbow and guiding her between the stacked plastic crates to the left of the doorway and the pile of galvanized tin baths to the right.

Once inside, Alice can barely believe her eyes. Her mouth open, she shakes her head and breathes, "Incredible!"

The store has a worn wooden floor, and a solid oak counter running from the front window to the rear wall. Alice runs her fingertips across the surface. Every square inch of the counter space is covered with miscellaneous hardware: tools, pots, pans, tubs; sawing, cutting, drilling equipment, and displays proffering varnishes, insecticides, penknives...

The rest of the store, to the left, looks more like a warehouse than a store. Boxes are piled high with only narrow alleyways between them, and from the ceiling coming down – as it were – to meet the boxes, are suspended gardening tools, horse-riding equipment, even a wheelbarrow.

Alice breathes deeply. "And that smell!" she exclaims. "What *is* that? Linseed oil? It's like something from *The Waltons* in here."

Will – who is weaving through the narrow passageways between the stacked goods – replies, "Isn't it fabulous! And you haven't seen the best bit yet! You haven't seen the secret attraction of Cole's Hardware."

"We stopped coming for a while," Jude says. "When we were broke. It's a bit more expensive than the big stores, but we love it here so much."

Alice shakes her head in wonder and follows them into the maze. "So what's the secret?" she asks. "What's the secret best bit?"

"Hello!" A voice booms out from the right hand side of the store.

Jude tips his head sideways indicating that Alice should follow, and weaves through to the counter.

"Well, if it isn't my favourite pair of fags!" the shopkeeper exclaims.

"Jess!" Jude says, taking his palm in a long warm handshake.

"Jude, Will," the man says, now noticing Alice's presence, and calming his buoyant tone. "Ma'am," he says, nodding at her deferentially.

Alice nods and, taking in the deep brown pools of his eyes, the gentle smile lines around them, and the general massiveness of his seven-foot frame, takes his hand. "Alice," she says.

"So how have you been?" Will asks.

Jess nods and grins. "Good," he says. "All the better now you guys are back and keeping me in business."

Alice looks at Jude who rolls his eyes. "Jess is lucky if we spend fifty dollars a month here," he explains.

She coughs. The man's regard is just a little too intense for her. "I was just saying what a beautiful store you have here," she says, feeling a little flushed. "It's like a museum." She suddenly thinks that that might not sound the way she means, so she adds, "Like a kind of museum to how life used to be, how life *should* be."

Jess nods and smiles warmly at her. "That's the way I try and live it," he says, crossing his arms and leaning on the worktop. He looks as if he is settling in, as if he has decided to watch her for some time.

Alice looks at his huge hands clasping his elbows through the plaid of his shirt. She opens her mouth to speak and then – forgetting what she was going to say – closes it again. She frowns and rolls her head from side to side rubbing her neck against the collar of her jacket.

Then, suddenly aware that Will and Jude have returned to the rear of the store, she points vaguely behind her and stammers, "I should really … go … help…" and turns.

With eye contact broken, Jess straightens and stretches before gently lifting a flap in the counter-top.

"So what can I *do you for* today, boys?" he asks, addressing the depths of the store.

"Tarp," Will's voice comes back. "Black tarp."

\*\*\*

As they climb into the pickup, Alice watches as Jude pushes his tongue against the inside of his cheek and grins saucily at Will.

"What?" she asks, both blushing and frowning.

Will shrugs and shakes his head. "Nothing," he says. "Nothing at all."

Jude guns the engine and pulls out onto the main street before asking, "So what do you think, Alice?"

"Oh, totally amazing," Alice says. "And such good smells! Awesome shopping experience."

"And Jess?" Will prompts, laughter in his voice.

Alice shrugs. "He seems sweet."

Will frowns, steals a glance at Jude and then frowns lopsidedly at Alice. "Sweet?" he asks. "*Sweet?*"

"*Hot* is more like it," Jude says.

Alice shrugs and nods simultaneously. "That too I guess," she says.

Jude is laughing. "He liked you," he says.

"Didn't take his eyes off you," Will adds.

"And did you see how quiet he went?" Jude says.

Alice frowns to herself. "I thought, he was, you know, ... *gay,*" she explains.

Will whoops. "Gay? Jess?"

"Honey, you need to attune your gaydar," Jude says, camping it up.

Alice nods. "Guess I do," she says. "I just thought, when he called you his favourite fags ... I guess I didn't think a straight guy would dare say that."

"Jess has bad habits," Will says. "It took him a while to get used to us. I think we were the first gay guys he ever knew socially."

"He's great though," Jude says. "He's our gentle giant."

"We love Jess," Will says.

Alice nods and runs her tongue across her lips, then settles back into her seat for the drive home.

After a minute though, Will nudges her with his hip. "Well?" he asks.

Alice blushes again, but pretends she doesn't know what he's talking about. "Well what?"

"Well what about it?" he says. "Should we invite him over while you're here?"

"Of course not!" Alice says, irritated.

"He comes to dinner all the time," Jude explains. "It would be the most natural thing in the world."

"Don't be silly," Alice says peevishly. "What would I possibly want with Jess?"

Will sniggers. "I know what I'd do with Jess."

"Given the chance," Jude adds.

Alice tutts and shakes her head.

"Think about it," Will says, his tone now serious.

"Will! He works in a hardware store. He lives … wherever that was… I mean, get real."

The cab falls silent, and they drive listening to the noise of the engine, the sound of the tyres on the highway.

After nearly half an hour, Alice is feeling nervous. "Have I said something I shouldn't?" she says. "I mean, I don't mean to…"

Will shakes his head and rubs her shoulder. "No, you're fine Alice," he says. "It's your loss."

Jude clears his throat. "I was just thinking how interesting it is. From a writer's point of view, I mean. To see you do what you do. To see it so clearly."

Alice nods. "I see," she says, then, "So go for it. *Share!*"

Jude snorts derisively and then shakes his head. "It's amazing really," he says. "I mean, you just met the hottest guy we know…"

"*Really!*" Will laughs.

"And he couldn't take his eyes off you."

"*Really!*" Will says again, with a nod.

"And in a single phrase, you…" Jude adds, turning from the highway, "you made him insignificant."

Alice frowns and turns to watch the countryside. She wonders if she can spot another fox.


After dinner, Alice heads through to Jude's study. He is sitting at his laptop.

"Jude?" she says, startling him.

He glances over his shoulder at her and then looks back at the screen. "Alice," he says flatly.

Alice sighs. "Look, I don't want there to be bad feeling, Jude. I'm sure your friend is lovely, it's just…"

"He lives in the wrong place and works in a hardware store," Jude says.

Alice coughs and shifts her weight to the other foot. "Well, yes," she says. "I guess."

Jude shrugs. "It's OK," he says.

"I do appreciate your honesty, you know," Alice adds. "I do hear you, you know. I do hear what you're saying to me, and I will think about it. And I am grateful. For the concern."

Jude shrugs again and then swivels to face her. He smiles. "That's OK," he says. "You're welcome."

Alice nods, shifts her weight again, and then starts to turn back towards the kitchen.

"Alice," Jude says, causing her to pause. "You're into poetry right?"

Alice nods. "Yeah," she says, relieved that, judging from Jude's voice, normality is restored. "You know I am."

"*Fall comes, with cold winds and grey skies...*" Jude recites. "*Mind struggles to hang on to the optimism of summer, with recompense of log-fires and potatoes, but we are not convinced, and dream of springtime.*"

Alice cocks her head to one side and stares at him. He is looking at her with a neutral, unfathomable expression. "Again?" she requests.

Jude repeats the lines.

*Fall comes, with cold winds and grey skies...*
*Mind struggles to hang on to the optimism*
*of summer,*
*With recompense of log-fires and potatoes,*
*But we are not convinced, and dream of springtime.*

Alice smiles gently, her eyes half-closed. "It's lovely, Jude," she says.

Jude nods and smiles. "I know," he agrees.

"I didn't know you wrote poetry," Alice says.

Jude snorts. "Jess wrote it," he says.

Her mouth slips into a restrained smile. "Jess wrote it," she repeats quietly.

Jude pushes his lips out and beams at her. "Jess wrote it," he says again. "Do you want to read the others?" He waves the manila folder at her.

Alice nods, smiles and takes it. "Thanks," she says.

"They're not exactly high art," Jude says. "He's no poet laureate, but they're always interesting. He has some good ideas."

Alice wanders through to the kitchen and opens the folder. A half sheet of paper falls out from the mass of pages. She turns it towards her and reads the handwritten words.

*So much choice in the city,*
*skipping from soul to soul.*
*Like too many TV channels,*
*frantically changing, ever dull.*
*Look for love, passion, joy,*
*well, you have to dig deeper.*
*Stop changing channels,*
*hunting more, better, sleeker.*
*Yes they move to the city,*
*to find stronger love, brighter friends.*
*But out here in the slowlands,*
*is where a heart mends.*

# Caravan Of Hope

Cheung perches on the edge of the cold stone wall and glances back at the shack to check that Lin is out of earshot. He thinks five is too young to really understand but just in case...

The air outside is cold and his breath hangs in the air – another winter heading their way.

"I want to talk to you," Juan said. He knows what she wants to say, and he knows that he will listen. Again. And then he will sleep on it and in the morning the spirits of the ancestors will have told him whether he should stay or go.

Juan takes a seat by his side and turns towards him; her face is less than a foot from his own. Around them the Sichuan night darkens, and their ears automatically attune for the sounds of animals. There have even been sightings of leopard cats, which – as concerned as they by the coming winter – seem every year to come closer to their village.

Juan flips the tail of her shawl behind her and reaches for Cheung's chin, applying the slightest pressure so that he looks her in the eye. "I know you are planning something," she says. "And I don't want you to go; not yet."

Cheung swallows hard and nods.

"The project people are coming soon. Mrs Zheng heard. It could be any day," she says. "So I don't want you disappearing on me."

"Project!" Cheung says quietly. He shakes his head. "You still believe the government will do something for us."

Juan nods. "Mrs Zheng says, and she always knows everything. Her son's very well placed in the Party. They are coming, with electricity and to build a school. And not the government, the Americans, the French – charity people."

Cheung raises an eyebrow. It's a woman's role to dream of a better life, to believe that things can change. And it's a man's role to assure survival, to take the hard decisions that need to be taken to make sure that they are alive, today and tomorrow and the day after.

"They need twenty good men from the village," Juan is saying. "A good builder like you…"

Cheung nods and listens and takes her sinewy hand, rough and calloused from her work in the fields. Every year there are rumours of something new, something different, but the government never does anything. The government can't even provide them with firewood.

"Maybe they will," he says, stroking her fingers. "Maybe Mrs Zheng is right, and they will arrive and build a school and make electricity. But what if they don't Juan? It wouldn't be the first time. And winter is coming, and Lin needs new shoes, and you need…"

"I need nothing," Juan interrupts. "Except you. And Lin needs her father."

Cheung nods calmly and smiles. "In Longhua, there will be work. There is always something in Longhua. I can send you money, like before.

"But you won't come back," Juan says. "They never come back."

Cheung runs his hand up Juan's sleeve, then releases her arm and slides a cigarette pack from his pocket. He pulls the final cigarette from the sleeve and fingers it, considering whether to smoke it now or save it for the journey.

"And if I don't go? All it needs is another winter like the last. And what if Lin gets ill?" he says. "What will we do then?"

"But you won't come back," Juan says again.

"I already did come back," Cheung says. "Why don't you trust me?"

"And if there is work here," Juan says. "If the project people come, how will I tell you if you are in Longhua? Tell me that."

Cheung shuffles sideways so that his thighs are touching his wife's. "OK, I will reconsider," he tells her, averting his gaze and sliding the cigarette back into the pack, and then the pack back into his shirt pocket.

"Come," he says, standing, reaching for Juan's hand and pulling her up. "She will be asleep now."

He leads her across and into the darkness of the shack, lifts his sleeping daughter and places her on the far side of the mattress, pulls off his shoes and slides carefully under the covers.

"You're not undressing?" Juan asks.

"Cold," Cheung whispers quietly. "I'm too cold tonight."

A hand reaches over and covers his mouth. Cheung awakens instantly from a light tormented sleep. "It's time," a voice whispers to his right.

Cheung lies for a moment listening to the sound of breathing beside him, takes in the sweet smells of the shack in an attempt to memorise them forever, then rolls carefully from the bed.

Outside, Sun Lee is waiting. Cheung pulls on his shoes, grabs his bag, hidden behind the hut, and, raising a finger to his lips to indicate silence, they creep away. Neither man speaks until they reach the track leading from the village.

"I'm glad you decided to come," his friend says.

Cheung pats him on the back and then looks across the mountainside where a halo from the imminent sunrise is starting to light up the horizon. Somewhere away to the right a parakeet shrieks.

"You think there is definitely work in Longhua?" Sun Lee asks quietly, the only other sound their feet, crunching on the gravel of the track.

Cheung shrugs. "There can't be less work than here."

"True enough."

"And the last time I found work quickly enough. In only two days. Even Juan got work in Longhua. It's where we met."

It takes about an hour to walk around the edge of the paddy fields and over the mountain track, and as they walk – their lungs smarting at the icy air – Cheung casts his mind back over the years; so much struggle to make ends meet, but with Juan and Lin, so much joy also. And now this; now they have to live apart again.

When they reach the junction, two men are already sitting cross-legged on the edge of the tarmac.

Sun Lee addresses them, saying, "Morning friends, you heading for Longhua too?"

One of the two men nods silently. "Yes, Longhua."

"No, Chongquuing," the second man says.

They sit beside them, and Cheung pulls the cigarette from his pocket. "It's my last," he says. "We share it huh? For luck."

The sky flames red now, and then shifts to pink and by the time the men have smoked the cigarette a dim vague daylight is spreading down the almost fluorescent green valley.

Cheung glances back up the track and shivers.

"You worried Juan will come and haul your arse back there?" Sun Lee laughs.

Cheung looks at him soulfully. "No. I think I may be *praying* for her to come and drag me back," he replies.

"Motorbike!" exclaims one of the men, and they all pause and strain their ears until they too hear the distant throbbing.

As the sound becomes louder, a spot appears over the distant hill. It bounces and bounds towards them.

As the bike nears, it slows, noisily crunching through the gears, and then finally stops in front of the group.

The rider, a plump man wearing Chinese army fatigues and no crash helmet pulls off his goggles and smiles at the four men who have crowded round.

"Where are you going, friend?" asks the older man. "You taking me east to Longhua? Is that it?"

The rider shakes his head slowly and grins broadly. "No," he says, pulling a sheet from his pocket. "Yaaja village," he reads.

"You're there, I mean, it's *here*," Sun Lee says, pointing at the gravel road running around the base of the mountain.

The rider peers behind him. "Tell the others," he says, revving the noisy engine and bumping off down the track. "Wave them down and tell them it's here," he shouts, gravel spitting from the rear wheel of the bike.

The other men sit back down but Cheung remains standing, frowning after the motorcycle.

"Don't worry," Sun Lee says. "Not Police."

Cheung shakes his head. "No," he says, breaking slowly into a smile. "Something else then."

"Trucks," the old man alerts them, and the four men stand again and peer at the horizon. A distant rumble, almost like thunder, and then a shimmering, and then suddenly they materialize, six, no, seven, no *eight* trucks lurching and bumping towards them.

Cheung turns, pulls at Sun Lee's sleeve, then releases it. "Come," he says. "Quickly."

It takes Sun Lee almost a minute to tear his eyes from the unlikely caravan, from the dust and the shimmering chrome pipes, and by the time he manages it, Cheung is thirty yards away, scrambling as fast as he can back up the mountainside.

"But Cheung," he shouts. "Where are you going?"

"Home," Cheung shouts back breathlessly. "I'm going home."

Also Available From BIGfib Books

# 50 Reasons to Say "Goodbye"

## A Novel by Nick Alexander

**Mark is looking for love in all the wrong places.** He always ignores the warning signs, preferring to dream, time and again, that he has finally met the perfect lover until, one day...

Through fifty different adventures, Nick Alexander takes us on a tour of modern gay society: bars, night-clubs, blind dates, Internet dating... It's all here. Funny and moving by turn, *50 Reasons to Say "Goodbye"*, is ultimately a series of candidly vivid snapshots and a poignant exploration of that long winding road; the universal search for love.

*"Modern gay literature at its finest and most original."*
Axm Magazine, December 2004

*"A witty, polished collection of vignettes... Get this snappy little number."*
– Tim Teeman, The Times

"Nick Alexander invests Mark's story with such warmth... A wonderful read; honest, moving, witty and really rather wise."
– Paul Burston, Time Out

### ISBN: 2-9524-8990-4
Available from www.BIGfib.com

Also Available From BIGfib Books

# Sottopassaggio

## A Novel by Nick Alexander

*I don't know how I ended up in Brighton. I'm in a permanent state of surprise about it. Of course I know the events that took place, I remember the accident or rather I remember the last time Steve ever looked into my eyes before the grinding screeching wiped it all out. It all seems so unexpected, so far from how things were supposed to be...*

**Following the loss of his partner,** Mark, the hero from the bestselling *50 Reasons to Say "Goodbye"*, tries to pick up the pieces and build a new life for himself in gay friendly Brighton.

Haunted by the death of his lover and a fading sense of self, Mark struggles to put the past behind him, exploring Brighton's high and low-life, falling in love with charming, but unavailable Tom, and hooking up with Jenny, a long lost girlfriend from a time when such a thing seemed possible. But Jenny has her own problems, and as all around are inexorably sucked into the violence of her life, destiny intervenes, weaving the past to the present, and the present to the future in ways no one could have imagined.

**ISBN: 2-9524-8991-2**
Available from www.BIGfib.com

Also Available From BIGfib Books

# Good Thing, Bad Thing

## A Novel by Nick Alexander

**On holiday with new boyfriend Tom, Mark – the hero from the best-selling novels, *50 Reasons to Say Goodbye* and *Sottopassaggio* – heads off to rural Italy for a spot of camping.** When the ruggedly seductive Dante invites them onto his farmland the lovers think they have struck lucky, but there is more to Dante than meets the eye – much more.

Thoroughly bewitched, Tom, all innocence, appears blind to Dante's dark side... Racked with suspicion, it is Mark who notices as their holiday starts to spin slowly but very surely out of control – and it is Mark, alone, who can maybe save the day...

*Good Thing, Bad Thing* is a story of choices; an exploration of the relationship between understanding and forgiveness, and an investigation of the fact that life is rarely quite as bad – or as good – as it seems. Above all *Good Thing, Bad Thing* is another cracking adventure for gay everyman Mark.

"Spooky, and emotionally turbulent – yet profoundly comedic, this third novel in a captivating trilogy is a roller-coaster literary treasure all on its own. But do yourself a favour, and treat yourself to its two prequels as soon as you can."
– Richard Labonte, Book Marks

**ISBN: 2-9524-8992-0**
Available from www.BIGfib.com

Also Available From BIGfib Books

# The Dark Paintings

## A Novel by Hugh Fleetwood

**Wealthy, depraved and hugely gifted, Luigi Teramo likes to think of himself as a cross between a pagan fertility God and an evil wizard.**

Luigi has deliberately rejected his youthful talent for art in favour of making money, and of spending his fortune on young men and drugs. But he cannot bring himself to destroy the fruits of that rejected talent – his early paintings. And as the years pass, it starts to seem that those paintings possess a terrible power. A power that will cause Luigi's life to spin out of control, will destroy almost all who get close to him, and will end by involving him in blackmail, and murder...

*The Dark Paintings* is both a thriller and a black comedy – entertaining, shocking and profoundly disturbing.

**"A tinge of the supernatural, a titillating whiff of the perverse, and – topping it off – a compelling miasma of creepiness..."**
– Richard Labonte – Books To Watch Out For

ISBN: 2-9524-8995-5
Available from www.BIGfib.com

Printed in the United Kingdom
by Lightning Source UK Ltd.
119689UK00002B/91-498